SHERLOCK HOLMES
MYSTERY MAGAZINE

#10 (VOLUME 4 NUMBER 2)   September/October 2013

FEATURES

NON FICTION

FICTION

CLASSIC REPRINT

ART & CARTOONS

"SO ENDS THE CASE OF THE GIANT HAT OF SUMATRA. UH, WATSON, WHEN YOU REFER TO IT IN YOUR WRITING PERHAPS YOU COULD CHANGE THE NAME A BIT TO MAKE IT SOUND A LITTLE MORE INTERESTING."

MARC BILGREY

Publisher: John Betancourt
Editor: Marvin Kaye
Assistant Editors: Steve Coupe, Sam Cooper

Sherlock Holmes Mystery Magazine is published by Wildside Press, LLC. Single copies: $10.00 + $3.00 postage. U.S. subscriptions: $59.95 (postage paid) for the next 6 issues in the U.S.A., from: Wildside Press LLC, Subscription Dept. 9710 Traville Gateway Dr., #234; Rockville MD 20850. International subscriptions: see our web site at www.wildsidemagazines.com. Available as an ebook through all major ebook etailers, or our web site, www.wildsidemagazines.com.

FROM WATSON'S SCRAPBOOK

Both Holmes and I are doubly delighted with this, the 10th issue of *Sherlock Holmes Mystery Magazine*. Firstly because, with the exception of one article and the usual columns by Mrs Hudson and Lenny Picker, all of the stories are about Holmes and me—all adventures and problems that until now I hadn't managed to write up.

Our second reason for rejoicing is that our magazine, which up to now has been published quarterly, now becomes a bimonthly periodical—which means, of course, that we shall be in need of more submissions!

No fewer than ten new Holmesian narratives appear below. I have restricted myself to a brief composition called "The Field Bazaar," though, for personal reasons, I have allowed my editorial colleague Mr Kaye to run it as if it had been written by Doyle, my literary agent. Of the other selections, I merely wish to comment favourably on one of them—"The Curse of Edwin Booth," which, having occurred on the other side of "the pond," I mean the Atlantic Ocean, I was not involved in it. But I am glad that Holmes has seen fit to assign its writing to Ms Carole Buggé, who already has done splendid renditions of two of our longer, hence novel-length, exploits, *The Star of India* and *The Haunting of Torre Abbey*.

And now I shall turn over the rest of this editorial column to Mr Kaye.

—John H. Watson, MD

Other than the good doctor's classic cases, *Sherlock Holmes Mystery Magazine* seldom runs reprints, but this issue makes an exception.

One of the interesting sidelights concerning Dr. Watson's many stories is the question of viewpointing. In all but three cases the tales are told first person by the good doctor himself. However, two of them—"The Adventure of the Lion's Mane," and, earlier, "The Adventure of the Blanched Soldier," which Dr. Watson is very fond of because in it, Holmes finally admits that he was wrong for frequently badgering his friend for "pandering to popular taste instead of confining himself to facts and figures." His exasperated companion finally dared him to "Try it yourself, Holmes!" and when he did so, the following admission was penned: "...I am compelled to admit that, having taken my pen in hand, I do begin to realize that the matter must be presented in such a way as may interest the reader."

The third story to vary from the first person style is "The Adventure of the Mazarin Stone"—the only tale in the entire Canon to be told third person! It came about in an unusual fashion. Its history was first written up by Watson's literary agent Arthur Conan Doyle—(Watson would prefer it if I added the prefatory title "Sir," but I look upon Death as the Great Leveler)—in the form of a one-act play titled "The Crown Diamond." According to anthologist Peter Haining, it was performed in London on May 16, 1921. William S. Baring-Gould says that "The Adventure of the Mazarin Stone" occurred on a summer's day in the year 1903. The question, of course, is who wrote it. Since it was composed third person, which Watson never chose to employ, I assume that it was adapted from its theatrical original by Doyle himself.

In this issue, two stories are not in first person. "The Curse of Edwin Booth" is told by the title character himself, whereas Zack Wentz's "Simplicity Itself" comes from one of those street urchins whom Holmes employed as part of his Baker Street Irregulars.

Our next issue will feature a new Holmes adventure transcribed by one of SHMM's best "regulars," Mr. Jack Grochot, as well as Watson's own "A Case of Identity." Other stories include ones by the following authors: Marc Bilgrey, Jay Carey, Sergio Gaut vel Hartman, G. Miki Hayden, D. Lee Lott, and Gary Lovisi.

Canonically Yours,

– Marvin Kaye

COMING NEXT TIME...

STORIES! ARTICLES!
SHERLOCK HOLMES & DR. WATSON!

Sherlock Holmes Mystery Magazine #11
is just a few months away...watch for it!

SCREEN OF THE CRIME

by Lenny Picker

A BAKER'S DOZEN OF PASTICHES THAT WOULD MAKE GREAT MOVIES

While it might seem that the market is currently glutted with film and TV interpretations of the Master, the Robert Downey movie series, BBC's *Sherlock* and CBS's *Elementary* all share a nontraditional take on Sherlock Holmes. Continued vigorous sales of DVDs of the Granada Jeremy Brett adaptations, and the original 60 stories, though, support the idea that there is still an appetite for in-period versions. And with Amazon and Netflix producing their own television series, and the likelihood that at least some of the above-mentioned series won't be around in five years, don't be surprised if before too long someone out there takes a crack at adding to the long and distinguished roster of actors who have played Holmes in more conventional plots and settings. But any such production would need a hook to attract investors. So, with a surfeit of modern-day Holmes, Downey covering the steam-punk possibilities of the character, and Brett, and especially BBC Radio's Clive Merrison having done the original stories, what's left?

Pastiche. While purists (and those who can't add) regard it as a four-letter word, for over a century (perhaps as far back as 1893, with J.M. Barrie's "The Late Sherlock Holmes"), many (count me among them, at least for the last four decades), have longed for stories faithful to the spirit and tone of the originals that provide further opportunities for gaslit streets, the urgent knock on the door of 221B, dazzling deductions and devoted comradeship. That's the route Bert Coules took after the BBC did the complete Canon for radio, with most of the stories adapted by Coules. (NB—my personal favorites—his version of "Dancing Men," with a very different, but extremely effective, opening, and a very compelling "The Final Problem"). In his *The Further Adventures of Sherlock Holmes*, Coules presented 15 new exploits, inspired by the dozens of Watson's tantalizing untold tales, such as Colonel Warburton's Madness and the politician, the lighthouse and the trained cormorant. (Perhaps his tour-de-force is "The Abergavenny Murder," in which Holmes and Watson solve the crime from their armchairs.) In doing so successfully, Coules proved, again, that in the right hands, pastiches can be both faithful and gripping.

With his gifts for adapting the Canon to a different medium, Coules would be the perfect choice to turn his talents—and perhaps the exploits he's already penned—to television or film. (He has stated that he has had a film script of *A Study in Scarlet* sitting around for quite a while.) But our hypothetical producers might look elsewhere, to print stories that would translate well to visual media. If I were to be asked, a prospect even less likely than Mycroft departing from his set routine to rescue Mary Morstan in a boat (sorry, *Sherlock Holmes: A Game of Shadows*) here, in no particular order, are some of the best written pastiches that should be seriously considered for adaptation.

The boom in such stories triggered by the success of the Royal Shakespeare Company's revival of the William Gillette play, *Sherlock Holmes*, and Nicholas Meyer's *The Seven Per Cent Solution*, gave the world many less-than-stellar stories that the world could have survived without. To cite but one example, one author's effort at Watsonian narrative voice included the line, "It was the beginning of that season the English so appropriately called winter." But there was gold amid the dross, especially Edgar Award winner Rick Boyer's first crack at the Canon, 1976's *The Giant Rat of Sumatra*.

Holmesians reasonably differ about the most intriguing of the adventures Watson never published, but for many, these lines in "The Adventure of the Sussex Vampire" stand alone:

"Matilda Briggs was not the name of a young woman, Watson," said Holmes in a reminiscent voice. "It was a ship which is associated with the giant rat of Sumatra, a story for which the world is not yet prepared."

Boyer was neither the first nor the last to attempt to flesh out this reference, but many agree that his novel is the best. His rodent of unusual size is responsible for a series of deaths in London and elsewhere that may be connected with a kidnapping in India. Chapter One, "The Tattooed Sailor," opens in the best Canonical tradition—"The summer of 1894 was hot and dry and without noteworthy cases or events, save for the mysterious disappearance of Miss Alice Allistair which threw the Kingdom into shock and sorrow." Boyer's especially good in raising the hairs on the back of his readers's necks, as in a scary sequence set in some dark woods where the monstrous creature may lurk. His Watson writes, "Never shall I forget the eerie spell which came upon me when I finally realized that I had been staring at Henry's Hollow for the previous ten minutes. Even as I write these words, I can once again feel the tremor of excitement that comes when witnessing something unique and grand." And as in the best stories, canonical or not, Boyer manages to touch the heart as well as the mind, doing so here in his account of a devastating fire on the docks, and the lives it claimed. "To call it fire would be an injustice. A slice of Hell, fetched up and planted on the river bank, would be a better description." (Boyer's *Giant Rat* has recently been reprinted by Titan Books as one of *The Further Adventures of Sherlock Holmes* series).

But excellence alone is not enough to make a pastiche screenworthy. Boyer's *Giant Rat* combines deduction and action in a manner reminiscent of *The Hound of the Baskervilles*, the most-filmed of the original 60, and the presence in the story of a monstrous creature only makes it more appealing. (Cave canem nocte: as readers of my first column know, successfully translating the demon dog of Dartmoor from the image conjured up on the page onto the screen has been difficult at best, and a scary enormous rodent might be even harder to pull off.)

A possible supernatural element is also present in another candidate worthy of the big or small screen, "The Secret of Shoreswood Hall," by Denis O. Smith, inspired by the legend of the Monster of Glamis, purported to be the hideously-deformed member of the nobility who was kept locked up in a hidden room. Smith is for my money one of the five best pasticheurs ever, despite his undeserved obscurity, even among Sherlockians, a status that will change, hopefully, with the 2014 publication of his *The Mammoth Book of the Lost Chronicles of Sherlock Holmes*. In his four volumes of *The Chronicles of Sherlock Holmes*, Smith demonstrated facility at both the Watsonian voice and the Holmesian brilliance, and was nimble enough to even emulate those Canonical stories that did not center on a corpse, a much more difficult challenge. His "The Adventure of the Willow Pool" is also a candidate for adaptation—it centers on an army captain, "who, on his return from the war in Afghanistan, is ignored and shunned by friends and acquaintances in his home village—where he has been liked and respected all his life." As with "Shoreswood Hall," "Willow Pool" is distinguished by clever, sophisticated plotting, a baffling puzzle that gives Holmes ample opportunity to impress, and spot-on characterizations.

2011 saw a lot of hype about Anthony Horowitz's *The House of Silk*, inaccurately called the first pastiche ever authorized by the Conan Doyle estate. But despite that puffing, Horowitz, best-known stateside for his *Foyle's War* TV series, delivered. A year after Holmes's death, Watson finally brings himself to recount events that "were simply too monstrous, too shocking to appear in print... it is no exaggeration to suggest that they would tear apart the entire fabric of society." That foreshadowing sets the bar high for the cases of The Man in the Flat Cap and the House of Silk, but Horowitz clears it, making it look easy, and leaving many hoping for another pastiche from his pen. He pulls off a variation of one of the most difficult opening scenes from the Canon—Holmes's seeming to read Watson's mind, this time commenting, "Influenza is unpleasant, ...but you are right in thinking that, with your wife's help, the child will recover soon." There are many scenes that cry out for a visual interpretation to supplement Derek Jacobi's stand-out audiobook. And Horowitz's skill set means that producers need seek no further for a screenwriter.

The late Barrie Roberts made a name for himself with nine novel-length pastiches published over a 13-year period. *Sherlock Holmes and the Man From Hell* (also a recent Titan reprint) uses a reference from the Canon to a matter involving a Lord Backwater as the springboard for a suspenseful mystery. What could be more evocative than a message received before a murder reading, "The man from the Gates of Hell will be at the old place at 6"? And that outing was no fluke; Roberts is one of the only authors, in my opinion, to succeed at a witchcraft-themed pastiche; *Sherlock Holmes and the Harvest of Death* features a plotline that offers ample bandwidth for the creative director to inspire fear with visual effects and a spooky soundtrack.

Speaking of visuals, is there a master-criminal more florid than Sax Rohmer's Fu Manchu? Fortunately, those who like their pastiches pitting Holmes against an evil mastermind can have their tastes sated by Cay Van Ash's *Ten Years Beyond Baker Street* (1984). Fu Manchu's traditional nemesis, Scotland Yarder Nayland Smith has disappeared, and Smith's medical sidekick, Dr. Petrie, turns to Baker Street for help.

Planting Holmes square in the midst of a ghost story inspired by a well-known Henry James story was a stroke of genius on the part of Donald Thomas in his *Sherlock Holmes and the Ghosts of Bly*. Time and again, Thomas has proven that he deserves a spot in anyone's top ten of all-time best pastiche writers, and his latest, *Death on a Pale Horse*, his first novel, gives Holmes a new potent adversary in a truly epic and continent-spanning case.

Want more suggestions, Mr./Ms. Director?

Carole Buggé also does ghosts justice in 2000's *The Haunting of Torre Abbey*, involving the spirit of a murdered monk. Fans of David Pirie's inspired Murder Rooms series, with the real-life inspiration for Holmes, Dr. Joseph Bell, brilliantly-portrayed by the late, lamented Ian Richardson (covered in detail in my column, *The NonSolitary Cyclist* in *SHMM* 3) will surely hope that his *The Dark Water*—another witchcraft-themed outing will someday hit the small screen, somehow with a lead not overshadowed by Richardson.

Like your Holmes films to feature travel beyond familiar London scenes? Then Michael Hardwick's *Prisoner of the Devil*, which plausibly injects Holmes into the Dreyfus Affair, would appeal.

John Taylor has added to the audio universe with two CDs of new stories—*The Unopened Casebook of Sherlock Holmes*, featuring spine-tingling radio plays such as "The Horror in Hanging Wood" that tore a man to pieces, and the Benedict Cumberbatch-narrated *The Rediscovered Railway Mysteries and Other Stories*, highlighted by "The 10.59 Assassin," Taylor's most challenging puzzle. (And Taylor has an untold tale of his own; reliable sources suggest that the intriguingly-titled *Sherlock Holmes: The Museum of the Impossible* may yet become a reality.) "The Horror in Hanging Wood" especially cries out for film treatment.

Finally, as an on-scream adversary for the Master, Jack the Ripper is at least second only to the Napoleon of Crime. Manly Wade Wellman and Wade Wellman's off-beat but effective *Sherlock Holmes: The War of the Worlds* opens with an authors's note commenting that the first Holmes-Ripper movie, *A Study in Terror*, was the only film they saw "in which the magnificent speed of Holmes's thinking [was] brought to life with full effect." That quality was also to the fore in the second Holmes-Ripper screen treatment, *Murder by Decree*, which suggests that Lyndsay Faye's *Dust and Shadow*, an extremely well-researched and historically faithful take on the Whitechapel Murders, would do well in translation. (Yes, that makes 14, not 13, but I wondered how many of you would read this column that closely.)

Readers may well have their own candidates for stories and writers—please feel free to email me at the address given below. If any of the above see the light of day on TV or in the theatres, I would be delighted. And as a die-hard pastiche devotee, who approaches new publications often out of hope rather than experience, I do wish that the concept I've suggested in-period pastiche films—does become a reality someday, even if their plots are completely new.

Lenny Picker has had his own pastiche "in the works" over several decades and two continents. He can be reached at lpicker613@gmail.com.

ASK MRS HUDSON

by Mrs Martha Hudson

Dear Mrs Hudson,

May I ask where you purchase your kitchen supplies in London? I don't mean the foodstuffs, but the dishware and related appliances, etc.? I am just setting up house for a newly-knighted Peer, and wish to do him proud!

Annalee Newitz

✗　✗　✗　✗

Dear Mrs Newitz,

At the risk of sounding rather traditional, I find that Harrods has most everything I need. Certainly the quality is reliable, and the selection is most agreeable. However, one does not always care to push through the considerable crowds found in such a large and popular store, and in such cases I visit a Chinese importer by the name of Mr Chen, who has a charming little shop in Limehouse. He is from Shanghai, and speaks only Mandarin, but the few words of English he knows are enough to make commerce with him quite agreeable.

In fact, I often prefer dealing with him, since I am able to avoid the mindless chatter British sales people often hurl at me while I am trying to decide what type of cheese cloth to purchase. I find it most annoying, and Mr Chen spares me such falderal, watching patiently as I sort through his wares to find what I need. He has the most marvelous pigtail, which he wears braided down his back—it reaches nearly to his waist. And his wife is quite beautiful—one of those Chinese women whose skin seems made of polished brass, it is so smooth and flawless. Her English is considerably better than his. Occasionally she offers me tea, and I feel quite honoured to share a pot of jasmine or lotus tea with her while her husband wraps the goods I have purchased.

Speaking of which, if you are in search of tea tins, certainly you should pay a visit to Mr Chen's shop. Harrods may do for everyday practical supplies, but if you wish to present your gentleman with something truly special, you must look through Mr Chen's selection of Chinese and Japanese wares. They are hand painted, and the one I bought has a lovely floral motif, and in the background one of those curved bridges you see in Oriental silk paintings. I also purchased the most ingenious spice box of Japanned tin—it has a gold border and radiating compartments. As you no doubt are aware, there is a great passion amongst society people for all things Oriental, and your peer will be most impressed with your ingenuity at finding such cunning objects.

If you do visit Mr Chen, please convey my regards. Tell his wife that Martha Hudson looks forward to taking tea with her soon.

Yours truly,
Mrs Hudson

✗   ✗   ✗   ✗

Dear Mrs Hudson,

I wonder whether you ever absorbed Mr Holmes make a mistake?

Geoffrey Clennam
Newcastle upon Tyne

✗   ✗   ✗   ✗

Dear Mr Clennam,

Mr Holmes rarely makes mistakes, though I perceive you have made one—that is, assuming you mean "observe" rather than "absorb." It is difficult to imagine absorbing a mistake, though I have no doubt certain Americans would prove me wrong.

But to be quite serious, yes, I have observed such a thing—it was, in fact, a curious and rather amusing incident. It was while he was recovering from the shock to his system engendered by his defeat of Professor Moriarty. He was having bad dreams—reliving that fateful day at Reichenbach, I think, though he never admitted it to me.

And so when I chanced to come upon him one morning in his sitting room, a tea tray in my hands, I concluded he had suffered yet another restless night. I observed him sorting through his collection of papers, all the while muttering to himself. The room was in unusual disarray, even for him, and judging by the beard stubble and puffy pockets beneath his eyes, I was fairly certain he had not slept at all. Mr Holmes was normally a most fastidious man, so when I saw him in that condition, I knew something was amiss

However, he ignored my inquiry as to his state of well-being (as he often did).

"Mr Holmes, are you quite well?" quoth I.

"Harrumph," quoth he (or something to that effect).

"I've brought your tea," I said.

He gave no answer, but tossed a few sheets of newspaper airborne, and stomped into the bedroom. I set the tray on the dining table and prepared to leave. I was stopped short by the sound of his voice from the next room.

"Mrs Hudson!"

With a sigh, I crossed to the bedroom and stood at the door, watching as he pawed through the contents on top of his bureau. "Yes, Mr Holmes?"

"Where the devil is the concert programme from last night?" he demanded, hands on his hips. He presented quite the picture, clad in his mouse-coloured dressing gown, his hair disheveled, a day's growth of beard stubble upon his chin. I almost burst out laughing, but the frazzled expression on his face stopped me.

"Well, Mr Holmes," said I, "I suppose it's wherever you left it when you came in last night. I was sound asleep at the time."

"Yes, yes, I know that—the question is, where did I leave it?"

"Perhaps it's in the pocket of your overcoat," I suggested.

"Capital idea." he exclaimed, brushing past me on his way to the front room. Seizing the garment from the bentwood coat rack, he rifled through the pockets, producing a crumpled programme from the Royal Albert Hall, which he and Dr Watson had attended the previous night. He held it aloft triumphantly. "Why, Mrs Hudson, I could kiss you!" he cried.

"That is quite unnecessary," I replied, blushing. Such effusions are so unlike Mr Holmes that it caught me quite off guard. "But perhaps you could tell me why that particular programme is of such importance to you."

"Ah! It is a matter of settling a bet," said he, eagerly scanning the text of the document.

My famous tenant had his vices, as is well known, but gambling was not one of them. "What sort of bet?" I inquired.

"The sort that one does not care to lose," he remarked.

I was afraid he had, in a moment of weakness, made a rash wager. "What is at stake?" I asked, rather fearing the answer.

"Dinner at the Savoy," he replied carelessly.

"Well, thank goodness for that!" I said, aware that perspiration had gathered on my brow. "I was afraid you had—"

He looked at me quizzically, then burst out laughing. "My dear Mrs Hudson—you thought I had—oh, really, that is too amusing!"

"Well," said I huffily, "it may be amusing to you, Mr Holmes, but since I rely upon your monthly rent, I assure you—"

"And you shall have it, and dinner at the Savoy as well!" he cried, pointing to the programme. The second half of the concert was devoted to the music of the American composer, Louis Moreau Gottschalk. His music was very popular in London at the moment, and I recognized the name. The list of pieces presented was printed in order, but the third line simply read, "To Be Determined."

"What does this have to do with—?" I began, but at that moment the door burst open and Dr Watson appeared, quite out of breath.

"'The Dying Poet!'" he exclaimed.

Mr Holmes frowned at him. "My dear fellow," he began, but Dr Watson cut him off.

"The composition we heard last night was 'The Dying Poet,'" he said, "not 'The Dying Swan!'"

"I still say you are wrong," Holmes rejoined.

"What does the programme say?" said Watson.

Holmes tossed it aside. "It is of no help whatsoever."

"I have just come from the Royal Albert Hall," Watson declared, "and they assured me that the piece Mr Balakirev played was indeed 'The Dying Poet.'"

Mr Holmes looked unconvinced.

"If you don't believe me, come along with me and hear it with your own ears," Watson insisted.

"That will not be necessary," Holmes replied stiffly. "I can rely upon your word."

"What is this all about?" I said.

"We attended a concert last night," Watson replied, "the second half of which was devoted to the music of—"

"Yes, yes, I know—Louis Gottschalk," I interrupted "What has a bet to do with all this?"

"In the back of the hansom cab afterwards Holmes insisted that the third piece was called 'The Dying Swan,' whereas I thought I recognized it as 'The Dying Poet.' So we made a bet on the spot—whoever was wrong would pay for dinner at the Savoy."

Holmes turned to me. "Will you do the honour of accompanying us, Mrs Hudson?"

I felt my face redden. "Why, Mr Holmes—"

"Oh, do come along, Mrs Hudson," Dr Watson said. "Otherwise I fear Holmes here will sulk the entire evening."

"If you insist," said I.

"Shall we say seven o'clock?" said Holmes.

"Very well," I replied. "And now I'd best be seeing about some eggs and sausage for your breakfast."

"Thank you, Mrs Hudson—I'm starving," said Dr Watson.

"And you, Mr Holmes?"

"I'm not hungry," he replied moodily.

I chuckled. "I daresay that will change when you inhale the aroma of a chive omelet and some lamb sausage."

And with that, I hustled myself downstairs into the kitchen, where I prepared a rather splendid breakfast, if I do say so myself.

It was not as splendid as the meal we dined on that night, however—oysters and game cock and blueberry pudding, with copious amounts of wine, ruby port and brandy for dessert. I woke up with quite the headache the next day, but it was worth it. Dr Watson told some stories of his combat days—we also found out how he came to know the music of Mr Gottschalk so well. It seems he had an encounter in medical school with a charming young lady from New Orleans, what the Americans might call a "Creole," and she played the piano quite credibly. 'The Dying Poet' was one of her favorites, and he declared he must have heard it a dozen or more times during the period he knew her.

None of this served to repair Mr Holmes's bruised pride, however—it was some time before he went to another concert with the good doctor.

And that is the story in its entirety, my dear Mr Clennam. I rather doubt it will appear in one of Dr Watson's tales, but I can still see the look of satisfaction on the good doctor's face. He had so few victories over Mr Holmes, that I have no doubt he especially savoured this one, trivial though it was. I personally think Mr Holmes was still rattled after his encounter with the Professor, hence his lapse of memory, but I did not say so at the time, preferring not to raise the spectre of his recently dead nemesis. You will perhaps agree with me that some things are better left unsaid.

Yours very truly,
Martha Hudson

ELDRITCH, MY DEAR WATSON

by Darrell Schweitzer

THE H.P. LOVECRAFT—SHERLOCK
HOLMES CONNECTION

"As for 'Sherlock Holmes'—I used to be quite infatuated with him!" wrote the horror master H.P. Lovecraft in a letter to his friend Alfred Galpin in 1918, "I read every Sherlock Holmes story published and even organized a detective agency when I was thirteen, arrogating to myself the proud pseudonym of S.H. This P.D.A. [Providence Detective Agency—DS]—whose members ranged between nine and fourteen years in age, was a most wonderful thing—how many murders and robberies we unraveled! Our headquarters were in a deserted house just outside of the thickly settled area, and we enacted, and 'solved,' many a gruesome tragedy. I still remember our labours in producing artificial 'bloodstains on the floor!!!' " (1)

As S.T. Joshi remarks in his monumental biography of Lovecraft, *I Am Providence*, this letter gives us one of the most pleasing glimpses of the young author, before the nervous "collapse" of his later teens, playing detective with the neighborhood kids, perhaps with a little more brilliance and determination than most—it is clear that Lovecraft was the leader in all this—but nevertheless behaving very much like a normal boy for perhaps the first and only time in his life.

Lovecraft went on in a letter to August Derleth in 1931:
"But I may remark that I, too, was a detective in my youth—being a member of the Providence Detective Agency at an age as late as 13! Our force had very rigid regulations, & carried in its pockets a standard working equipment consisting of police whistle, magnifying glass, electric flashlight, handcuffs (sometimes plain twine, but "handcuffs" for all that!), tin badge, (I have mine still!!!), tape measure (for footprints), revolver, (mine was the real thing, but

Inspector Munroe (at 12) had a water-squirt pistol while Inspector Upham (at 10) worried along with a cap-pistol) & copies of all newspaper accounts of desperate criminals at large—plus a paper called The Detective, which printed pictures and descriptions of outstanding "wanted" malefactors.... We shadowed many desperate-looking customers, & diligently compared their physiognomies with "mugs" in The Detective, yet never made a full-fledged arrest. Ah, me—the good old days!" (2)

It is just as well that Detective Lovecraft a.k.a. "S.H.," did not show off his quite genuine pistol while stalking a suspect. Those were indeed more innocent times, when parents did not think too seriously about letting their 13-year-old play with a real pistol, even one which was (presumably) in less than working order.

This great fascination with Sherlock Holmes and with mystery fiction was, quite clearly for Lovecraft, a phase. In both letters, the larger context is a discussion of juvenile tastes and former habits. Lovecraft's fascination with detective stories was not restricted to the Sherlock Holmes stories either. He read an enormous amount of general pulp fiction between about 1905 and 1914, including virtually every issue of *Argosy* and *All-Story* during this period, which contained much detective fiction. As a child he had been by all indication an avid reader of dime-novels and other juvenile mysteries of the period (some of which was published in a format similar to a modern comic book, although mostly text), following the exploits of Nick Carter, King Brady, and other largely-forgotten heroes. Many of his earliest attempts at fiction were detective stories of a sort, such as "The Mystery of the Grave-yard" (1898 or 1899, i.e., written when Lovecraft was eight or nine) which is nothing less than a miniature dime-novel, with very short chapters, some no more than fifty words.

But, certainly as he grew a little older, Sherlock Holmes was his favorite, and he definitely (as is clear from his letters) read the first three Holmes novels, and the collections *The Adventures of Sherlock Holmes, The Memoirs of Sherlock Holmes,* and *The Return of Sherlock Holmes.* He did not read the later Canon, as far as we can tell, ever. He read some of Doyle's supernatural work, though affording him no more than one sentence, a longish sentence in "Supernatural Horror in Literature," singling out

"Lot No. 249" and "The Captain of the 'Pole-Star'" for praise. Overall, despite his dismissing Doyle's later Spiritualist writings as "senile drivel," Lovecraft seems to have regarded the author of the Sherlock Holmes stories as a very competent storyteller, and particularly good reading for younger folks.

But detective fiction, by and large, was something he felt he had outgrown as he reached adulthood. In a 1929 letter to Derleth he expresses doubt that S.S. van Dine's Philo Vance would have much appeal for him, remarking, "I hate these laboriously whimsical & artificially mannered fiction-heroes—they are so mechanical that these lose all touch with reality & become grotesque bores." (3) He does promise to look into Father Brown sometime, though there is no indication he ever did. In other letters, mostly to persons other than Derleth, he expresses less than complete enthusiasm for Derleth's detective novels, although he does courteously praise Derleth's Holmes-pastiche Solar Pons series.

If it were merely the case that H.P. Lovecraft enjoyed the Sherlock Holmes series in his youth and then lost interest, there would be no point in writing this article. The only question is what this circumstance—the early enthusiasm for Holmes on the part of HPL—means.

Essentially, Lovecraft and detective fiction had a philosophical parting of the ways. In 1914, as a result of letter exchanges between Lovecraft and other readers in the pages of *The Argosy*, Lovecraft discovered amateur journalism, and for the first time in his life came into wide contact with other literary-minded persons. This broadened his tastes and outlook enormously. But more to the point, Lovecraft's interest had always been toward the cosmic. Another of his boyhood obsessions was astronomy, and it was the intensive study of this subject, together, no doubt, with the experience of staying up nights peering into the depths of infinity through his telescope that convinced Lovecraft that, ultimately, mankind had only a very small, even trivial role to play in the cosmos at large. As if that were not enough, at precisely this time astronomers had just determined that those swirling "nebulae" they had been observing were in fact other galaxies, made up, not of clouds of gas, but of billions of stars, and located much further away than previously thought. So, if anything, the depths of infinity had just gotten considerably larger.

For Lovecraft, then, the fascination (and the aesthetic attraction) was in the vast sweep of time and space. He sought the cosmic in fiction, in his own and in what he read. Lovecraftian horror stems largely from the characters's realization of their own helpless and trivial role in the cosmic scheme of things. It is as if anyone could say abstractly that the history the Earth might be written out as a 300-volume encyclopedia, and the history of mankind occupies only the bottom half of the last page—but Lovecraft genuinely felt this. As a consequence, for all he might admire Holmes's brilliance and rationality and the deft artistry of the Doyle stories, which clearly stood for him head and shoulders over most other such fiction, the actual plots of detective stories failed to hold his interest.

In that same 1931 letter to Derleth, a couple of paragraphs earlier, he had explained, "I never acquired an interest in the peep-show contrasts & ignominies empirically classified as 'scandal'—perhaps because of a cosmic perspective which felt no vast difference betwixt one sort of inane behavior and another sort of inane behavior on the part of terrestrial puppets." (4) In other words, if organic life itself is to be seen, as Lovecraft saw it, as a chemical-electrical phenomenon which may have occurred briefly on one particular fly-speck planet in a vast and chaotic universe, then it didn't particularly matter who politely poisoned whom in an English country-house or made off with milady's jewels. The mature Lovecraft didn't find mere crime to be of sufficient dramatic interest.

So the matter narrows down to what Lovecraft carried away from his youthful Sherlock Holmes enthusiasm. Things we do or read in childhood do go on to shape the adults we become, even if we "outgrow" them. Scholar Peter Cannon has written about the Holmesean influence on Lovecraft at some length. There are the motifs and the parallel passages, as to be expected, and one easily recognizes the source of the spectral, baying creature in Lovecraft's story "The Hound."

But it's more than that. What would have appealed most to Lovecraft, and remained consistent with his philosophical outlook throughout his life, was Holmes's rationality, as summed up by the Great Detective's famous statement (in "The Adventure of the Sussex Vampire") that "This Agency stands flat-footed upon the ground…. No ghosts need apply." Holmes is making an explicit rejection of the supernatural, or at least of his interest in it. "The world"—meaning the material plane—is "large enough" for him.

Lovecraft, too, completely rejected the supernatural in any "spiritual" sense. There are no ghosts in his fictions. Human beings, who are bio-chemical phenomena of random Nature, have no "souls." Even in "The Case of Charles Dexter Ward," which deals with the resurrection of the dead, this resurrection is achieved by material means, a matter of "essential salts" collected from the dust of the grave and processed through arcane alchemy. His monsters, Cthulhu, Nyarlathotep, et al., are immensely powerful cosmic beings, the products of a broader universe of which mankind knows virtually nothing, but they are not "gods" in the traditional sense.

Lovecraft, as quite a small child, was sent home from Sunday school when he started asking embarrassing questions about how, if Santa Claus and the Easter Bunny are imaginary, the Judeo-Christian deity is not likewise imaginary. He was entirely unable to accept the "Semitic mythology" in which he was expected to believe. This was an attitude which stayed with him for his entire life. To him, nothing was more absurd than the sentimental notion that any sort of cosmic creator would notice or care in the slightest about the doings of creatures on our particular planetary flyspeck.

You will notice how many Lovecraft stories resemble detective stories in their structure. "The Call of Cthulhu" details a methodical, inexorable investigation which assembles clues and leads the protagonist to a terrible conclusion. The other key Holmes observation which must have impressed Lovecraft is the one repeated several times throughout the Canon, that once all other possibilities have been eliminated, what remains, however improbable, must be the truth.(5)

Try as they may to avoid doing so, Lovecraftian characters inevitably work out that, yes, a gigantic squid-faced being has indeed been sleeping for millions of years under the Pacific and waits to claim the Earth again, or that there are indeed winged Fungi from Yuggoth in the Vermont hills, or that one Joseph Curwen of Providence, Rhode Island (died, 1771) has actually managed to return to life after more than a century in the grave and impersonate his hapless descendant, Charles Dexter Ward, or that the rural disturbances collectively known as "The Dunwich Horror" are caused by the appalling interbreeding between Yog Sothoth and a human disciple, and this threatens to end the world as we know it.

Lovecraft did not go in much for continuing investigator characters, but subsequent writers quickly picked up on the obvious implications. He was certainly familiar with such "psychic detectives" as William Hope Hodgson's Carnacki or Algernon Blackwood's John Silence. Dr. Willett in "The Case of Charles Dexter Ward" or Professor Armitage in "The Dunwich Horror" and most especially Police Inspector Legrasse, who figures in "The Call of Cthulhu" very easily could have, having concluded one "case" that averted cosmic menace, gone on to devote the rest of their careers to such activities.

August Derleth quickly produced one Laban Shrewsbury, who stars in a whole series of Lovecraftian adventures (*The Trail of Cthulhu* et al.) and the contemporary writer C.J. Henderson has written an entire volume of subsequent investigations of Legrasse (*The Tales of Inspector Legrasse*). Surely more writers will continue in this mode in the future. Even Peter Cannon, scholar, humorist, and pastichist, has produced a tale, *Pulptime*, in which Lovecraft, his friend Frank Belknap Long, and an aged Sherlock Holmes actually meet in the 1920s and share an adventure together.

What Lovecraft was doing, then, was applying the Holmesean method to the universe at large. He had dispensed with the small stuff—human crime—and taken on a larger subject—the frightful position of mankind in a vast and uncaring cosmos over which we have no control, but his characters proceed with the same logical, step-by-step deduction that Holmes used for mundane matters, until they arrive, not unflinchingly, we will admit, but still arrive, at the same thing that Holmes was after: the truth, however mind-blasting it might be.

That's what the grown-up H.P. Lovecraft, late of the Providence Detective Agency, was after all along.

He knew Holmes's methods, and applied them, not to human crime, but to the haunted-house gulfs of cosmic infinity.

NOTES:

(1) H.P. Lovecraft. *Letters to Alfred Galpin*, p. 19.
(2) H.P. Lovecraft. *Essential Solitude*, p. 323.
(3) H.P. Lovecraft. *Essential Solitude*, p. 203-204.
(4) H.P. Lovecraft. *Essential Solitude*, p. 322.
(5) For instance, "Eliminate all other factors, and the one which remains must be the truth," from *The Sign of the Four*. In *The Annotated Sherlock Holmes*, p. 613. Note 26, p. 614, lists numerous further expressions of the same sentiment in other stories.

SOURCES:

Cannon, Peter. "Parallel Passages in 'The Adventure of the Copper Beeches' and 'The Picture in the House.'" *Lovecraft Stories*, Vol. 1 No. 1 (Fall 1979), pp. 3-6.

_____. "You Have Been in Providence, I Perceive." *Nyctalops* #14 (March 1978), pp. 45-46.

Joshi, S.T. *I Am Providence, The Life and Times of H.P. Lovecraft*. (2 vols). New York: Hippocampus Press, 2010.

Lovecraft, H.P. *Letters to Alfred Galpin*. Edited by S.T. Joshi and David E. Schultz. New York, Hippocampus Press, 2003.

Lovecraft, H.P. and August Derleth. *Essential Solitude, The Letters of H.P. Lovecraft and August Derleth* (2 vols.) edited by David E. Schultz and S.T. Joshi. New York: Hippocampus Press, 2008.

SHERLOCK HOLMES AND SCIENCE FICTION

by Amy H. Sturgis

Detective fiction and science fiction are siblings of a sort. Both are descended from the Enlightenment's faith in a systematic, comprehensible universe. They even share a parent. Edgar Allan Poe not only created fiction's first detective of note, C. August Dupin, in "The Murders in the Rue Morgue" (1841), "The Mystery of Marie Rogêt" (1841), and "The Purloined Letter" (1844), but he also served as a key voice in early science fiction. A quick glance at the table of contents of Harold Beaver's edited collection *The Science Fiction of Edgar Allan Poe* (1976) reveals stories dealing with mesmerism, galvanism, resurrection, and even time travel, among other concepts, following the trail blazed by Mary Shelley and anticipating Jules Verne, H.G. Wells, and other stars in the science fiction constellation. These authors posed the question of "what if?" and extrapolated from contemporary scientific knowledge to offer imaginative answers spiced with the flavor of plausibility.

Despite the close relationship of the genres, it's a rare character who moves back and forth comfortably between the two. Sherlock Holmes, however, has made a lasting home in both the detective and science fiction literary worlds. Understanding why Holmes has appealed to science fiction audiences and how he has been incorporated into the science fiction canon yields useful insights into the Great Detective's lasting popularity.

CONAN DOYLE, HOLMES, AND THE SCIENCE FICTION SENSIBILITY

During his forty-five years as a writer, Arthur Conan Doyle published works in a wide variety of genres, non-fiction and fiction, from historical romance to contemporary politics. It is worth noting that before, while, and after achieving fame with the Sherlock Holmes novels and stories, Conan Doyle also wrote science fiction. There is no one "science fiction moment" in his career; on the contrary, he maintained a life-long involvement with the genre.

For example, the publication of his "The Great Keinplatz Experiment" (1885), a tale about personality exchange, predated the introduction of Holmes in *A Study in Scarlet* by two years. After *A Study in Scarlet* and *The Sign of the Four*, and in the same year as the debut of the first collection of Holmesian short stories, *The Adventures of Sherlock Holmes* (1892), Conan Doyle published both "The Los Amigos Fiasco" and *The Doings of Raffles Haw*. The former tells the story of how a condemned criminal gains superpowers when subjected to an experimental electric chair; the latter explores a chemist's transformation into an alchemist who discovers the secret of transmuting lead into gold.

Two years later, his novel of telepathic vampirism, *The Parasite*, followed. In 1910, well into the phenomenal success of his Sherlock Holmes works, Conan Doyle published "The Terror of Blue John Gap," a short story about a monstrous creature who lives underground. Two years after the release of the final Sherlock Holmes stories came *The Maracot Deep* (1929), Conan Doyle's novel of the discovery of Atlantis by a deep-sea scientific expedition. This list is hardly exhaustive. Over the decades Conan Doyle also produced a number of other stories that could be considered to have science fiction elements, as well.

Perhaps his greatest achievement in the genre remains his works centered on the scientific jack-of-all-trades known as Professor Challenger. Just as Conan Doyle drew on his own real-life mentor Joseph Bell to create Sherlock Holmes, he modeled George Edward Challenger on another figure he knew from the University of Edinburgh: Professor of Physiology William Rutherford. Between 1912 and 1929, Conan Doyle published three novels (*The Lost World*, *The Poison Belt*, and *The Land of Mist*) and two short stories ("When the World Screamed" and "The Disintegration Machine") in the series, pitting the larger-than-life Challenger against such forces as dinosaurs surviving on a remote plateau in South America, a poisonous band of ether fated to intercept the

Earth, and a brilliant technological invention with the potential to become a most dangerous weapon. The Challenger stories remain popular—and the inspiration for various pastiches—today.

SHERLOCK HOLMES AND THE SCIENCE FICTION SENSIBILITY

Given Conan Doyle's relationship to the genre, it should come as little surprise that the four novels and fifty-six short stories that comprise his Sherlock Holmes canon are infused with a "science fiction sensibility." Consider, for example, how John Watson initially hears of Sherlock Holmes from Stamford in the first Holmes novel, *A Study in Scarlet*. Stamford describes Holmes as "a little too scientific for my tastes—it approaches to cold-bloodedness." Stamford goes on to characterize the man as the sort who might, "out of a spirit of inquiry," use his friend—or, for that matter, himself—as a test subject for experimentation, due to his "passion for definite and exact knowledge."

When Watson first encounters Holmes in person, in the chemical laboratory of St. Bart's Hospital, he describes the scene in this way:

> Broad, low tables were scattered about, which bristled with retorts, test-tubes, and little Bunsen lamps, with their blue flickering flames. There was only one student in the room, who was bending over a distant table absorbed in his work. At the sound of our steps he glanced round and sprang to his feet with a cry of pleasure. "I've found it! I've found it," he shouted to my companion, running towards us with a test-tube in his hand. "I have found a reagent which is precipitated by hæomoglobin, and by nothing else." Had he discovered a gold mine, greater delight could not have shone upon his features.

In short, the reader's introductions to Holmes represent him with the single-minded zeal of a scientist in the familiar setting of a scientist. He is portrayed as a cerebral hero, one whose goal is not to conquer a land, win a girl, or defeat a villain, but rather to know. And, as the reader discovers along with Watson, Holmes employs his own disciplined method with exact precision in order to achieve this goal. His drive to understand, to solve the mysteries of the universe through methodical rationality, reveals Holmes as a distinctly science fictional protagonist.

Others agree. For instance, E.J. Wagner, whose book *The Science of Sherlock Holmes: From Baskerville Hall to the Valley of Fear, the Real Forensics Behind the Great Detective's Greatest Cases* recounts how Holmes influenced generations of forensic scientists in the same way that Star Trek later influenced physicists and engineers, says, "Sherlock Holmes may have been fictional, but what we learn from him is very real. He tells us that science provides not simplistic answers but a rigorous method of formulating questions that may lead to answers. The figure of Holmes stands for human reason, tempered with a gift for friendship."

Ryan Britt, in "Sherlock Holmes and the Science Fiction of Deduction," published in the science fiction publication *Clarkesworld Magazine*, seems to concur: "Essentially, Holmes believes any mystery can be approached, and a solution deduced, scientifically, by gathering necessary data, and drawing conclusions based on logic and reason. In the Doyle stories, the science of deduction usually always works, and serves as the basic premise for every single Holmes adventure. Like a science fiction writer, Doyle seemed to start with the premise of 'what if?'."

If the Holmes canon as a whole represents a science fiction sensibility, specific stories within the series qualify as science fiction proper. The most obvious, perhaps, is the 1923 short story "The Adventure of the Creeping Man." In this tale, an aging professor attempts to rejuvenate himself for his young bride by taking a drug derived from the langur monkeys of the Himalayas. Of course he does not realize that this concoction will alter both his body and mind, devolving him into a sinister, threatening figure. The flavor of the tale invites comparisons with other classic science fiction works such as Robert Louis Stevenson's *Strange Case of Dr Jekyll and Mr Hyde* (1886) and H.G. Wells's *The Island of Doctor Moreau* (1896).

Arguably an even better example from the Holmes canon is 1910's "The Adventure of the Devil's Foot." Holmes hypothesizes that the victims went mad and/or died from inhaling the powdered root of an African plant that, once heated, vaporizes and carries on the air. He tests the hypothesis on himself—so successfully that

Watson must save him, in what is one of the duo's most harrowing moments. Conan Doyle created the fictional plant at the heart of the mystery, but he presents it as plausible fact, going so far as to offer its scientific name (*radix pedis diabolic*, or "devil's-foot root" in Latin) for the sake of realism. Holmes builds and tests his theory of the crime like a proper scientist. As the genre legend Isaac Asimov admits in his introduction to *Sherlock Holmes Through Time and Space*, "The Devil's Foot" is not merely a compelling mystery, it is also "very good science fiction."

Since the Sherlock Holmes canon as a whole displays a science fiction sensibility, and some Holmes stories in particular are clearly works of science fiction, it is unsurprising that science fiction authors who came after Conan Doyle have chosen to use Sherlock Holmes in their own genre writings.

SHERLOCK HOLMES IN SCIENCE FICTION LITERATURE

During his lifetime, Conan Doyle opened Sherlock Holmes's universe to other creative minds. In an often-quoted telegram to U.S. actor and playwright William Gillette, he said this of his most famous character: "You may marry him or murder him or do whatever you like with him." Friends such as J.M. Barrie (of Peter Pan fame) wrote Holmesian stories for Conan Doyle's amusement. In the decades following Conan Doyle's death, the Holmes pastiche has become a popular phenomenon of its own. Within this tradition, a number of subgenres have developed, from Sherlock Holmes-meets-Jack the Ripper tales to romance stories in which Holmes finds true love.

One of the more popular of these subgenres often walks the borderline of science fiction. Stories in which Holmes encounters vampires may lean toward fantasy or science fiction, depending on how the vampirism itself is explained. What is certain is that some of those who have contributed to this Holmes-vampire subgenre are writers who have made their professional names in science fiction. For example, Fred Saberhagen, most famous among science fiction readers for his Berserker saga, also penned a series about Dracula comprised of ten novels and two short stories; *The Holmes-Dracula File* (1978) and *Séance for a Vampire* (1994), in particular, are noteworthy as Holmes pastiches. Best known for his Chronicles of Amber novels, Robert Zelazny combined Sherlock Holmes with Count Dracula and a host of other Victorian heroes and villains for *A Night in the Lonesome October* (1993), which was nominated for science fiction's prestigious Nebula Award.

A host of other writers have devised strategies for drawing Holmes into works that are undeniably science fiction. These may be divided into three loose categories: tales that fold Holmes into preexisting science fiction stories; tales that pair Holmes with various science fiction-related individuals, either fictional or historical; and tales that allow Holmes to travel in time or have other science fictional adventures. Discussing all such publications thoroughly would require a book-length study, but a few representative works may illustrate each of these approaches.

PAIRING HOLMES WITH SCIENCE FICTION-RELATED CHARACTERS INCLUDING HOLMES IN PREEXISTING SCIENCE FICTION STORIES

One trend in Holmes pastiches is that of retelling a well-known science fiction story, or offering a sequel to one, and including Holmes as a central character. For instance, the father-son writing team of Manly Wade Wellman and Wade Wellman published *Sherlock Holmes's War of the Worlds* in 1975. This novel—a collection of several short stories, more accurately, beginning with "The Adventure of the Martian Client," which first appeared in *The Magazine Of Fantasy and Science Fiction* in 1969—serves as a sequel to H.G. Wells's 1898 science fiction classic *The War of the Worlds*. It follows Holmes and Watson (as well as Conan Doyle's Professor Challenger) as they experience the Martian invasion of London. Titan Books released a new version in 2009 as *The Further Adventures of Sherlock Holmes: The War of the Worlds*.

Loren Estleman provides another example with his 1969 novel *Dr. Jekyll and Mr. Holmes*, which details how Holmes, at the Queen's request, investigates the murder of Sir Danvers Carew.

Holmes thus is drawn into the world of Robert Louis Stevenson's 1886 science fiction novella *Strange Case of Dr Jekyll and Mr Hyde*. (This, too, was rereleased by Titan Books in 2011.) The formula continues to be popular; Guy Adams's 2012 work *Sherlock Holmes: The Army of Doctor Moreau* builds upon *The Island of Doctor Moreau* by H.G. Wells (1896), enabling Holmes and Watson to discover the chilling experiments conducted by Wells's brilliant-but-mad physiologist.

PAIRING HOLMES WITH SCIENCE FICTION-RELATED CHARACTERS

A second kind of story pairs Holmes with characters, either historical or literary, who are associated with traditional science fiction. Take, for example, *The Shadow of Reichenbach Falls* (2008) by John R. King. This novel picks up where Conan Doyle's Holmes story "The Final Problem" ends, at the bottom of Reichenbach Falls, adding a new element: Thomas Carnacki. Carnacki, known as the "Ghost Finder," starred in multiple short stories by William Hope Hodgson from 1910-1948. One of science fiction's earliest "paranormal investigators," Carnacki utilized both contemporary technology (such as photography) and imaginary technology (such as his beloved "electric pentacle") when on a case. King employs Carnacki to save Holmes and then team up with the Great Detective against Professor Moriarty in an adventure with decidedly supernatural overtones.

Similarly, Barbara Roden pairs Holmes with another classic genre character in her short story "The Things That Shall Come Upon Them" (first published in *Gaslight Grimoire* in 2008). Created by Hesketh V. Hesketh-Prichard (a friend of Conan Doyle's) and his mother Kate, writing as E. and H. Heron, Flaxman Low was science fiction's first "psychic detective." Stories featuring Low appeared in *Pearson's Magazine* and, in 1899, were published together in the collection *The Experiences of Flaxman Low*. In her tale, Roden contrasts Holmes's and Low's quite different approaches to solving mysteries when she assigns both detectives the task of investigating the home of Julian Karswell from M.R. James's "Casting the Runes" (1911).

This approach also remains popular. In 2012, Howard Hopkins edited *Sherlock Holmes: The Crossovers Casebook*, offering stories that pair Holmes with a number of historical and literary characters, including Conan Doyle's own science fiction star, Professor Challenger.

ALLOWING HOLMES TO DO SCIENCE FICTIONAL THINGS

Other authors give Holmes science fiction-related adventures. For instance, David Dvorkin in *Time for Sherlock Holmes* (1983) posits a Holmes who has discovered the secret to immortality thanks to his bees and a Moriarty who has stolen H.G. Wells's time machine. As Moriarty travels into the future to assassinate world leaders and create chaos, the deathless Holmes (along with equally immortal John Watson and Mycroft Holmes) is there to meet him. Their conflict extends not only into future centuries, but into space itself as humankind explores the universe and colonizes the planets.

Nebula and Hugo Award winner Vonda N. McIntyre offers a more Earth-bound tale in her short story "The Adventure of the Field Theorems" (first published in *Sherlock Holmes in Orbit* in 1995). In fact, this narrative hits very close to home, as it has Arthur Conan Doyle himself consider the mystery of crop circles along with Holmes and Watson. Scientist Stephanie Osborn brings Holmes into the present day through her ongoing "Displaced Detective" series (including *The Arrival* and *At Speed* in 2011 and *The Rendlesham Incident* in 2012). In these novels, a modern-day female physicist discovers the alternate reality in which Holmes is doomed to die at Reichenbach Falls, rescues the detective, and brings him into our universe to share her high-tech adventures.

Several collections of Holmesian science fiction showcase how noted genre authors use Holmes in their works. Among the best of these are *Sherlock Holmes through Time and Space* (1984), edited by Isaac Asimov, Martin Greenberg, and Charles Waugh; *Sherlock in Orbit* (1995), edited by Mike Resnick and Martin Greenberg; and *The Improbable Adventures of Sherlock Holmes* (2009), edited by John Joseph Adams.

SHERLOCK HOLMES IN THE WORLD(S) OF H.P. LOVECRAFT

Writers and readers of Holmesian science fiction seem to agree that the Great Detective appears especially at home in the universe of one author in particular: H.P. Lovecraft. Lovecraftian Holmes pastiches—or is that Holmesian Lovecraft pastiches?—form an impressive literary presence of their own.

Why H.P. Lovecraft?

H.P. Lovecraft was a U.S. author of so-called "weird fiction" whose writings are recognized today as formative works in the development of contemporary science fiction, fantasy, and horror. He is perhaps best remembered as the father of the "Cthulhu Mythos," a shared universe of stories to which many writers contributed, inspired by the premise of Lovecraft's 1928 story "The Call of Cthulhu" and his related writings. "The Call of Cthulhu" suggests that alien creatures once ruled the Earth and in the future will awaken from their current slumber to reclaim their dominion. The insignificance of humanity on this indifferent cosmic stage threatens the sanity and lives of those people who are sensitive enough to perceive it.

At first blush, the otherworldliness of Lovecraft's vision might not seem a fitting subject for Holmes's skeptical attention. As Holmes himself says in "The Adventure of the Sussex Vampire" (1924), "This agency stands flat-footed upon the ground, and there it must remain. The world is big enough for us." No Great Old Ones from outer space, one might say, need apply.

There are, however, excellent reasons why so many authors have felt compelled to invite Holmes into Lovecraft's world(s). For one thing, the setting fits. Conan Doyle and Lovecraft were contemporaries; Lovecraft outlived Conan Doyle only by seven years.

Lovecraft was an enthusiastic Anglophile, as well, and fancied himself a Victorian gentleman by nature, if not in circumstance. Thus Lovecraft's writings reflect a certain flavor, a mood created by gaslight and shadows and veiled peril, that complements the tone of the Holmes canon well.

The message of both the Holmes stories and Lovecraft's work also agrees in principle: the universe is knowable. Conan Doyle's Holmes reaches his conclusions via the science of deduction. Lovecraft likewise constructed the body of his tales on the skeleton of the hard sciences. A serious study of astronomy, in particular, informed his mechanistic materialist views and led to the cosmic outlook of his fiction. The two authors drew different lessons from the comprehensibility of the world around them, however. The universe is knowable, Conan Doyle seems to tell readers, and is that not reassuring? We may find order in the apparent confusion. On the other hand, Lovecraft implies that the universe is knowable… but understanding it might drive one mad. (It bears repeating that Lovecraft's protagonists are often sensitive, thoughtful, curious scholars and researchers and investigators, all of whom suffer from the desire to know—not unlike Sherlock Holmes himself.)

Many readers see the appeal in bringing Conan Doyle's and Lovecraft's conclusions to bear on one another. In other words, blending their universes offers the chance to "shake up" the unflappable Sherlock Holmes at last, and/or the opportunity to bring a calming reason to Lovecraft's bleak and terrifying nightmares. Furthermore, as Lovecraft's stories are far more popular today than they were during his lifetime, especially within science fiction circles, writers who wish to write a Holmesian story feel comfortable in invoking Lovecraft's mythos, knowing they are safe in assuming some knowledge and familiarity on the part of readers.

EXEMPLAR WORKS

One example of a key Holmesian-Lovecraftian work is P.H. Cannon's *Pulptime. Being a Singular Adventure of Sherlock Holmes, H.P. Lovecraft, and the Kalem Club*, as if narrated by Frank Belknap Long, Jr (1984). This mystery involves Lovecraft himself as a character, as well as his writer friends who formed the "Kalem Club" (including award-winning author Frank Belknap Long), and Harry Houdini. Added to this blending of historical figures is the Great Detective himself: elderly, but instantly recognizable.

2003's *Shadows Over Baker Street: New Tales of Terror!*, edited by Michael Reeves and John Pelan, draws attention to this phenomenon by collecting some of the most compelling short stories that place Holmes in Lovecraft's universe. Science fiction and detective fiction author Barbara Hambly in "The Adventure of the Antiquarian's Niece," for instance, pairs Holmes and Watson with Carnacki the Ghost Finder to traverse the landscape of several of Lovecraft's stories, most notably "The Dunwich Horror" (1929) and "The Rats in the Walls" (1924).

Perhaps the single most famous Holmes-Lovecraft mashup also appears in *Shadows Over Baker Street*; it is Neil Gaiman's "A Study in Emerald," which won the Hugo Award for Best Short Story and the Locus Award for Best Novelette, both science fiction honors. This piece relocates Conan Doyle's "A Study in Scarlet" to the darker world of Lovecraft's Cthulhu tales.

The formula continues to yield new works. Christian Klaver's *The Adventure of the Innsmouth Whaler* (2010), for example, puts Holmes and Watson on a case directly related to Lovecraft's story "The Shadow Over Innsmouth" (1931). It is not uncommon to see Lovecraft-inspired works in the pages of *Sherlock Holmes Mystery Magazine*; the two lead stories in the June 2012 issue of *The Lovecraft eZine* are Sherlock Holmes stories.

The pairing even has leapt beyond fiction. The adventure game *Sherlock Holmes: The Awakened*, developed by Frogwares for Microsoft Windows in 2006, follows Holmes and Watson as they investigate mysterious disappearances linked to the Cthulhu universe. After drawing a worldwide audience (and winning GameSpot's "Best Use of a License" Award in 2007), a remastered version appeared in 2008. It earned not only popularity, but a rating of M (Mature 17+)—the first Holmes-related game to do so.

SHERLOCK HOLMES AND OTHER SCIENCE FICTION MEDIA

Sherlock Holmes has made himself as comfortable in other forms of science fiction media as he has in novels and short stories. A thorough review of his appearances demands a separate study, but a quick overview proves the point.

SHERLOCK HOLMES AND DOCTOR WHO

The world's longest-running science fiction television series, the BBC's *Doctor Who* (1963-present), has spawned several tie-in publications that feature Holmes. Andy Lane's novel *All-Consuming Fire* (1994) teams Holmes and Watson with the Seventh Doctor against Azathoth (one of the figures from Lovecraft's mythos). Two years later, in Paul Cornell's novel *Happy Endings*, Holmes and Watson are brought forward in time to attend the wedding of the Seventh Doctor's companion, Bernice "Benny" Summerfield, to Jason Kane. One of the novels in the Faction Paradox series, itself a spin-off to *Doctor Who*, is Kelly Hale's 1994 *Erasing Sherlock*, in which a doctoral candidate goes back in time, posing as a housemaid in 221B Baker Street in order to study the young consulting detective.

SHERLOCK HOLMES AND STAR TREK

Holmes's presence in "the final frontier" is, thanks to Nicholas Meyer, Star Trek canon. Holmes fans know Meyer first and foremost as the author of three pastiche novels, *The Seven-Per-Cent Solution* (1974, which was adapted to film in 1976 with Meyer's screenplay), *The West End Horror* (1976), and *The Canary Trainer* (1993). Star Trek audiences know him an uncredited co-writer for *Star Trek II: The Wrath of Khan* (1982), a credited co-writer for

Star Trek IV: The Journey Home (1986), and the co-writer and director of *Star Trek VI: The Undiscovered Country* (1991).

The parallels between the rational Holmes and Star Trek's logical science officer, Mr. Spock, became a running theme in Star Trek fan discussions and fan works almost from the first appearance of Trek on U.S. television in 1966. The fact that actor Leonard Nimoy, who brought Spock to life, also portrayed Sherlock Holmes in the documentary short *Sherlock Holmes: Interior Motive* (1975), and again in the 1975-1976 Royal Shakespeare Company's U.S. production of William Gillette's play *Sherlock Holmes*, invited further comparisons. As Nicholas Meyer told Ryan Britt (as cited in "Sherlock Holmes and the Science Fiction of Deduction"), "The link between Spock and Holmes was obvious to everyone. I just sort of made it official."

Meyer made it official in *Star Trek VI: The Undiscovered Country*. During a scene in which Spock puts forth his own deductions, he quotes directly from Conan Doyle's "The Adventure of the Beryl Coronet" (1892) and credits Holmes as a forefather: "As an ancestor of mine once said, 'Once you have eliminated the impossible, whatever remains, however improbable, must be the truth.'"

Star Trek: The Next Generation paid homage to both Holmes and the Holmes-Spock (and, by implication, Spock-Data) by having the android Data develop a taste for Holmesian roleplaying. Complete with deerstalker and pipe, Data faces off against a holographic version of Professor Moriarty in the episodes "Elementary, My Dear Data" (1988) and "Ship in a Bottle" (1993).

SHERLOCK HOLMES AND OTHER TELEVISION

Holmes has starred in other science fiction television fare, as well. For example, the made-for-television CBS movie *The Return of Sherlock Holmes* (1987) features Watson's present-day descendant Jane discovering a cryogenically frozen Holmes and reviving him. Perhaps the best example of the science fictional "updating" of the Holmes canon stories is the 1999-2001 animated series *Sherlock Holmes in the 22nd Century*, a co–production by DiC and Scottish Television. Each episode revisits classic adventures, with a twist:

the year is 2104. Sherlock Holmes, frozen for years, has thawed and returned to his detective work, joined by a robotic Watson and a descendant of Inspector Lestrade. Professor Moriarty is represented in this future by one of his clones.

THE BBC'S SHERLOCK

The most faithful and sophisticated reimagining of Holmes at present, and arguably one of the best adaptations of the Holmes canon at any time, the BBC's *Sherlock* (2010-present) displays a keen science fiction sensibility. This is to be expected, considering that co-creator Steven Moffat is also the head writer and executive producer of *Doctor Who*, and co-creator Mark Gatiss has written for and guest starred in *Doctor Who*, adapted for television and starred in H.G. Wells's *The First Men in the Moon* (2010), and performed in the live television remake of the science fiction classic *The Quatermass Experiment* (2005), among other genre-related accomplishments.

Although the series has displayed many science fictional characteristics since its debut (thoroughly exploring and exploiting contemporary technology, from blogs to mobile phones to government surveillance equipment), the second-series episodes "The Hounds of Baskerville" and "The Reichenbach Fall" (2012) qualify as science fiction proper. The former updates the Gothic fear of a spectral hound, recasting it in terms of conspiracy theories surrounding genetic experimentation at the Baskerville military research base to create a "luminous" super attack dog. Sherlock, John, and Lestrade uncover a conspiracy regarding ' H.O.U.N.D.,'' a secret government project designed to create a chemical weapon that triggers violent hallucinations in those exposed to it. The latter episode finds Jim Moriarty with a computer code capable of overriding any and all security systems, which he demonstrates by simultaneously opening the vault at the Bank of England, unlocking the cells at Pentonville Prison, and breaking into the display case containing the Crown Jewels.

The third series of the program, currently scheduled for filming in 2013, likely will continue to illustrate the affinity between the Holmes canon and science fiction.

SHERLOCK AND SCIENCE FICTION

In Conan Doyle's *The Hound of the Baskervilles* (1901-1902), Sherlock Holmes notes, "We balance probabilities and choose the most likely. It is the scientific use of the imagination." This is an elegant description of what Conan Doyle did, and what creators today continue to do, with Holmes. It is also an excellent characterization of the endeavor of science fiction itself: "the scientific use of the imagination." As today's world continues to blur the lines between science fiction and science fact, the Great Detective will remain as relevant and meaningful as ever, incorporated into the genre, figuratively and sometimes literally immortal.

✗ ✗ ✗ ✗

Amy H. Sturgis earned her Ph.D. in intellectual history from Vanderbilt University and is scholar of science fiction/fantasy studies and Native American studies, the author of four books and editor of six others. Her official website is amyhsturgis.com. This essay is based on a live lecture presented in February 2012 and sponsored by the Hugo Award-winning podcast StarShipSofa.

✗

THE ADVENTURE OF THE DOCKLANDS APPARITION

by Mark Wardecker

When trying to select which of my friend Sherlock Holmes's cases to lay before the public, I have often had to take consistency into account. For it was not unusual, given the many puzzles and problems with which he was presented, that a client's story might seem to contain those elements of the unique and even grotesque that Holmes found so gratifying, only for the case to later evaporate into the banal and the commonplace. Often, the most absorbing investigations began humbly, with a detail that seemed just slightly awry, such as a discarded photograph of a lady found lying upon the ground. And not since our encounter with the notorious Irene Adler had a photograph of a beautiful woman posed such a threat to a nation's stability as the one in the case I am about to relate.

It was on a gloomy, rainy day in the spring of 1896, just after Holmes and I had finished lunch, when Mrs Hudson entered our sitting room to announce Mr August Pierpont, a tall and sturdy man with greying sideburns and mustache.

"I am sorry to interrupt your meal, Mr Holmes and Dr Watson. If you like, I can return later, but circumstances have become unnerving enough that I felt I should waste no time in seeing you."

As Holmes regarded the man's flushed countenance and agitated respiration, he smiled slightly and replied, "Of course, Mr Pierpont, I would be happy to hear about these circumstances which have so unnerved you. Please, have a seat by the fire and tell us your story from the beginning. Watson, please pour our guest some brandy to calm him, and Mrs Hudson, those dishes can wait. Please make yourself scarce." Holmes took a seat by the fire and relit his pipe as he waited for our indignant landlady to depart and for our guest to sit down.

"Now, Mr Pierpont, please proceed. I realise that you will need to be getting back to the bank soon."

"But, Mr Holmes, how could you know?"

"It is simplicity itself. Your frock coat and trousers are of the very best black broadcloth, yet they have become somewhat shiny in the back, suggesting a job that requires you to remain sedentary for long periods. The slight stoop in your shoulders also marks you as a man who spends most of his time hunched over his desk. The pink corner of the *Financial Times* in your inner pocket suggests that you have something to do with finance, and the traces on the fingers and thumb of your right hand of that rosin that is frequently used by people who spend a great deal of their time counting money is also suggestive. Finally, that small, gold ornament depending from your fob with the initials, "IBE," engraved upon it is conclusive: you are employed by the Imperial Bank of England on Lombard Street. As I noted before, you are too well dressed to be a clerk, but I know you are not the director or branch manager of that particular establishment. I would venture, though, that you are in a position of some authority."

"I am an accounts manager for the Imperial Bank. That is uncanny, Mr Holmes!"

"Please, state your case," replied Holmes as he leaned back into his armchair and assumed the weary, heavy-lidded expression which veiled his keen and eager nature.

"Well, Mr Holmes, it may be as nothing, but three days ago an odd series of seeming coincidences began to unfold before me. I am a bachelor and own a small house in Christopher Street, Finsbury. As I was leaving for work Monday morning, I noticed what appeared to be a piece of litter lying on the stoop outside my front door. When I attempted to sweep it aside with my foot, it clung there stubbornly, so I knelt to pick it up. Mr Holmes, it was a photograph of a woman."

Fishing in one of his waistcoat pockets, Pierpont retrieved a small photograph of the most striking women I had ever seen. Raven-black hair framed a delicately and perfectly proportioned face of almost porcelain complexion, and there was an intensity in her dark eyes that gave the photograph an extraordinarily lifelike quality.

"The back of the picture is still slightly tacky with adhesive," observed Holmes. "May I keep this?"

"Of course. I only kept it on the off chance that I might bump into its subject in the neighborhood and return it." As he said this, a flush once again returned to his countenance.

"You do not know the subject?"

"I had never seen her before then, Mr Holmes. But on my way to work that morning, just as I was entering the bank, I saw her standing just outside a jeweler's, five doors down. I could not help but stare, and as I stood there trying to determine if it was, in fact, the same woman, she turned and seemed to recognize me. She took a step toward me, but I then lost sight of her as a passing throng of young clerks passed by. I stood there, like a fool, for some time but was unable to spot her again."

"So you are unsure that it was the same woman?"

"I was, Mr Holmes, but the thing that is so extraordinary is that I have seen her several times since. As you have noted, I do not have much opportunity to stretch my legs at the bank, and I try to walk as much as possible. However, on Monday evening, I worked rather late and decided to take a cab home. But just as I was putting the key in the front door of my home, I saw her again. She was walking toward me, and I had just caught sight of her before she turned into an alley three houses down from my house. I could hardly believe my eyes and immediately turned to follow her, but when I turned into the alley, there was no sign of her. Yesterday, I saw her again, both as I was arriving at and departing from work, and again, she vanished as suddenly as she appeared."

"Did she appear near the jeweler's yesterday, as well?"

"Yes, in that vicinity. I was relating the events to two of the clerks at work, and one of them joked that it sounded like a case for Sherlock Holmes.

"For lunch, I decided to take advantage of the break in the rain and walk to the George and Vulture. As I turned into Birchin Lane, there she was again! She was on the opposite side of the street and walking in the opposite direction. It did not look as though she had seen me, so I followed her, sticking to the opposite side of the road. We made our way almost as far south as Cannon Street before an omnibus passed between us, and I lost sight of her."

"Could you tell whence she had come?" asked Holmes.

"No, she seems to appear and vanish like a ghost. I could stand no more and immediately resolved to hail a cab and, all jesting aside, consult you."

"Your story contains elements that intrigue me, Mr Pierpont, but I am afraid that there is not yet a sufficient amount of data with which to work. I do promise to assist you, if necessary, in this matter and will ask you to please leave me your card and home address. Do not hesitate to contact me if anything else of significance happens. Watson will see you to the door."

With that, I led our guest back out and reassured him as he donned his hat and coat that Holmes would do everything in his power to help and that he should not worry about imposing upon us in the future. When I returned to our sitting room, Holmes was still sitting with his feet upon the fireplace fender, puffing away at his oily, black clay pipe.

"It is remarkable the lengths to which an old bachelor will go having caught sight of a pretty face," I remarked.

"A phenomenon with which you are no doubt familiar," retorted Holmes, smiling.

"Well, to be fair, if her photograph does her any justice at all, I probably would not object to walking after her in the rain, either."

"Then you shall have your chance. I have a small matter to attend to in the morning. I was hoping you would follow Mr Pierpont to work tomorrow morning and report back to me everything that you see," said Holmes as he stood and handed Pierpont's card to me.

I assured Holmes that he could rely upon me, and next morning found me standing half a block from the banker's neat, three-storey home in Christopher Street. It had stopped raining but a cold, damp fog had settled heavily upon The City, and when I saw Pierpont hail a cab, I immediately did the same, taking care not to be seen by him. On the way from his front door to the hansom, I noticed no change in his behavior, and we traveled slowly but without incident to Lombard Street. As he alighted from the cab, however, Pierpont turned dramatically and stared intently to his right. I quickly left my cab and tried to follow his gaze but could only see hoards of clerks, businessmen, and workmen all rushing about their customary early morning business in The City. Pierpont began to look rather wild and rushed down the street. Trying to be discreet, I was at a disadvantage as I followed him, but I was certain that, if our mysterious lady were somewhere in Lombard Street, I would surely have seen her. After having gotten about halfway down the block, I turned quickly into a tobacco shop as Pierpont returned dejectedly to the bank. Once he was out of sight, I continued to reconnoiter, but I never did glimpse the black-haired woman from the photograph.

I had just finished lunch when Holmes returned to Baker Street, and I related to him all that had occurred that morning.

"I am sorry I don't have more for you, Holmes."

"Not at all. Your professional opinion may be of value here. Did Pierpont seem...healthy to you...compos mentis?"

"Actually, Holmes when I saw the change in his features as he got out of the cab, I did become concerned. But of course, under the circumstances, there is no way to be certain about the state of his mind."

"No, but it is, at least, another possibility. But what is this?"

A frantic banging at the front door had begun, and soon, above Mrs Hudson's protestations, I could hear rapid footsteps on the stairs. Looking even more worryingly frantic than before, Mr Pierpont burst into our quarters.

"Mr Holmes, I saw her again! And she led me straight to a murder!"

"A murder? Mr Pierpont, this is really most grat...fascinating. Please, take off your coat and have a seat. Have you informed the police?"

After helping the banker out of his coat and pouring a drink, we sat down to hear his story.

"I have told Inspector Lestrade, who is the detective in charge. He told me he would wait for you at the scene of the crime."

"Then we must not keep him waiting. Please, from the beginning."

"Since I was unable to go yesterday, I thought I would walk to the George and Vulture for lunch today. Again, as I turned the corner into Birchin Lane, I saw the woman from the photograph on the other side of the street, heading in the opposite direction. This time, given the fog, I resolved to take no chances. I darted across the street, and after miraculously emerging in one piece onto the other side, I commenced to follow her. I was bolder this time, but she did not turn around as we headed south, past Cannon Street and, eventually, past Upper Thames Street. However, I was afraid she did spy me as she pivoted on her heel and quickly turned into a side street. Afraid of losing her, I quickened my pace and managed to catch up again before she turned into another, even narrower alley. It seemed remarkable that she wouldn't have spotted me as we wove through these tiny, dirty thoroughfares. Though I was unfamiliar with the neighborhood, I could tell we were still bearing south in an extremely roundabout way. And as crumbling tenements gave way to even seedier pubs and sooty warehouses, I could also tell we were getting very close to the Thames. I determined finally to call out to her, because I was truly concerned for her safety as I saw sailors, dockworkers, and assorted riffraff leering at her out of the fog. But just as I opened my mouth to yell, we suddenly emerged onto the docks, the Christopher Docks, to be precise and as I later learned.

"She never said a word, Mr. Holmes, but abruptly stopped and stepped to one side, looking toward two figures on the dock who were barely visible in the dense riverside fog. I was unprepared to stop and came within less than ten feet of the two men before halting. To my surprise, one of them was another accounts manager from my bank, a Mr Lewis Owen. He was on his knees and seemed to be unconscious. The other man, who was unknown to me, had a hold of Owen from under his arms, a truncheon still gripped in his right hand. I called Lewis's name, barely realizing what I was doing, but it was too late. The ruffian had already swung him around and pushed him into the river. The murderous brute then turned upon me, brandishing the truncheon, and I'm ashamed to say, I turned and ran faster than I have ever run.

"I had gotten no further than two blocks from the docks before seeing a constable and calling for help. My pursuer, however, had abandoned the chase and had disappeared back into the fog. The constable and I rushed back to the dock to help poor Lewis, but all we saw of him, upon returning, was his top hat floating in the water. I told him my story and repeated it to Inspector Lestrade when he arrived on the scene."

"And what did our friend, Lestrade, make of the affair?"

"He seemed to think it was merely a mugging that had gone too far."

"And his thoughts on the woman?"

"He appeared uninterested."

"Typical. I don't suppose you saw what happened to her?"

"No, Mr Holmes. She was gone when I turned to run."

"And the assailant's appearance?"

"He was about my height in rough brown tweed and a mis-shapen brown bowler. His face, what I could make out, was clean shaven. He was a little remarkable looking in that his mouth was rather long, almost reptilian looking, and he had either no or very thin eyebrows."

"This is really most interesting," remarked Holmes with that keen look in his eyes that always preceded the hunt.

"I don't know. What if I have been beset by a spirit from the other plane, sent as a harbinger of doom and disaster? Dear God! What if I should continue seeing her?"

"Please restrain yourself, Mr Pierpont. That you were being led somewhere is certain, but we must confine ourselves to physical entities of a far more commonplace type. How well did you know the victim?"

"Not very. He began working at the bank about five months ago, replacing Peters when he left unexpectedly. I know that he did good work, but he kept mostly to himself. He never mentioned a family or anything about his social life."

"Please think. Is there anything to connect you with Owen?"

"I'm sorry, but I can think of nothing. We worked in the same bank but never exchanged anything more than the most casual of greetings."

"Do you know if he was friends with any of the other employees?"

"Not that I am aware of. He came to the bank promptly every morning and departed by himself in the evening."

"All right, Mr Pierpont. Are you returning to the bank now? Good. Watson and I need to meet with Lestrade while there is still a chance his men have not entirely obliterated every scrap of evidence from the scene. We will stop by the bank afterwards."

Holmes and I took a cab to the Christopher Docks, and the ride was made interminably long by both the fog and by Holmes having fallen into one of his fits of reticence. Upon disembarking from the cab, once we had arrived at our destination, a smile returned to his face as he addressed our old comrade, and occasional rival, Inspector Lestrade.

"Greetings, Lestrade! I hear you have met one of my clients."

The cold, dirty fog was even denser here by the river, and it really did feel like we were on a different plane, with the shades of policemen, sailors, and stevedores hovering around us. Lestrade peered at us through the mist.

"It seems you are one step ahead of us this time, Mr Holmes. But never you worry. We'll close the gap before long."

"I have every faith."

"So, have you learned anything relevant from your client?"

"To be honest, I sent him on his way yesterday, because there seemed too little to go on. All that had happened were his continual encounters with the woman in this photograph," said Holmes, handing the picture to Lestrade. "You may keep that."

"Thank you, Holmes. He told us about his series of run-ins with the lady. At first, I thought them insignificant, but now I'm not so sure."

"What has made you change your mind?"

"It seemed, at first, like a routine mugging in a dangerous area, but then, a few moments ago, when he overheard me mention that the poor fellow worked for the Imperial Bank, one of the other detectives mentioned that that bank's director is at present being done for embezzlement."

"You don't say."

"Now I'm wondering if Owen were somehow involved in this mess?"

"You know, Holmes," I interjected, "you said something earlier about Pierpont being led here. What if the woman was trying to lead him here to prevent this from happening?"

"It's a leap. Pierpont isn't the first person to whom I would turn for protection, but leaps of the imagination are crucial in situations like these. Have your men found the body?"

"No, just Owen's hat floating in the river. I've already requested some boats to drag for him, but it will probably be some time before they get here, given the weather."

"I don't suppose there were any witnesses?"

"Here? The lads are talking to people, but I wouldn't hold my breath."

"May I take a look?"

"By all means," replied Lestrade and handed Holmes a bull's-eye lantern, for despite its being mid-afternoon, it was becoming quite dark.

After closely examining the bricks of the docks for several minutes, Holmes returned the lantern.

"Do you have anything to add, Holmes?" asked Lestrade.

"Only that the ground corroborates Pierpont's account, nothing more than we already know. There is a fine layer of mud that has been disturbed which could be indicative of a struggle, but there is no way of making out any prints. There are also some clothing threads that match his description of the subject. If you find the body or get anything out of the director, please let me know."

"And where are you headed?"

"To the bank for now. Tomorrow, I shall try to learn more of Mr Lewis Owen. I'll let you know if I find anything of interest."

We returned to our awaiting cab and proceeded north to Lombard Street and the Imperial Bank. When we arrived a short time later, the disruption caused by the director's arrest was still very much in evidence as both staff and patrons milled nervously about the large, marble lobby and desperate sounding clerks attempted to placate frightened sounding customers. Evidently, the arrest had already reached the newspapers. We entered a doorway to the left and walked down a narrow, wainscoted hallway to Pierpont's office. As we reached his door, he was just ushering out a skeptical looking older man, asserting repeatedly that the client's investments were perfectly safe. He seemed glad of any distraction and invited us in. Before entering, Holmes stopped to examine a photograph that hung on the wall.

"It is a picture from our last annual Christmas party," offered Pierpont.

"Is Owen in it?"

"Why, yes, he is. Right...here."

"May I borrow it?"

Pierpont looked at Holmes dubiously and then shrugged.

"I don't suppose, at present, that anyone will miss it," he said sighing.

After sitting down in some plush, leather armchairs before Pierpont's large, mahogany desk, Holmes asked the banker if he had been able to discover anything more about his murdered coworker.

"I'm sorry, Mr Holmes, but in all of today's chaos, I haven't had time to talk to anyone about him. As soon as things settle down, I shall try to learn more."

"That is perfectly understandable given the circumstances. There is one point on which you can probably enlighten me, however. Would Owen have been in a position to discover your director's embezzling?"

"Well, Mr Holmes, without yet knowing the exact circumstances, it would be hard to say. Obviously, he, and I for that matter, have access to the records of every account, including those of the director. If funds were being misappropriated in such a way that it would be discoverable from those records, then he could conceivably have uncovered what was going on. I must say, however, that I would hope a bank's director, even a crooked one, would be a little more clever."

"Thank you. If you find out more, please let us know. I shall be in touch."

As Holmes and I made our way back through the crowd in the echoing lobby, I attempted to sound him out.

"Not very much to go on, is it?"

"I shall certainly need more data. It is a capital mistake to theorize without data, and I doubt we shall be able to gather more until tomorrow. What do you say to dinner at Simpson's?"

That was as much about the case as I was able to get out of Holmes that evening, and after dinner, during which Holmes spoke at length about Vergil's *Georgics* and the light that work shed upon the qualities of bees, we returned to Baker Street. I turned in early and awoke shortly after dawn but found that Holmes had already departed. I heard nothing from him that entire day until a telegram arrived in the early evening:

"Come to the Diogenes Club at 6:30 if convenient. If inconvenient, come all the same."

Fortunately, I was available and so not overly annoyed at Holmes's summons. I arrived at that curious club where members are forbidden to speak or to take the least notice of each other. I was then ushered by a servant into the Stranger's Room, the only room in which guests and conversation were permitted. Holmes had already arrived and stood to greet me. Another man began to laboriously lift himself from his chair, and I recognized him even before he had turned around to greet me. Mycroft Holmes, Sherlock Holmes's older brother, was of considerably greater girth than his sibling, but he possessed the same keen, steel-grey eyes as his brother. According to Holmes, Mycroft's deductive and reasoning powers exceeded his own, and the specialism he provided his employer, the British government, was no less than "omniscience." Mycroft was also a founding member of this peculiar club and, when not at his lodgings in Pall Mall, could invariably either be found here or in Whitehall. After we had all exchanged greetings, we sat down, and Holmes began to address us.

"Your timing is excellent, Watson. I was just recounting the events of the past few days to brother Mycroft and just arrived at my breakthrough today at Somerset House. That is where I spent the entire day, going through the records of several of the government offices that are housed there. I was hoping there would be something—a will, an insurance policy, anything—that might shed some light on our missing banker."

"But Holmes, Owen isn't really missing. He's no doubt lying at the bottom of the Thames," I argued.

"No, Watson," he said smiling, "even when we were at the docks yesterday, I had serious doubts that a murder had actually been committed. The whole scenario seemed too obviously staged. The appearance of the photograph and the woman, the way she contrived to get Pierpont to follow her, it reminded me of other such cases. You noticed yourself yesterday that Pierpont was being led. Why? Was he being led away from The City so that a crime could be perpetrated, just as Hall Pycroft was led away from Mawson & Williams or Jabez Wilson was led away from his pawnshop in the affair of the red-headed men? Or was it to lead him to somewhere, possibly to witness a crime, like John Scott Eccles when he visited Wisteria Lodge? The elaborate tableau at the scene of the crime and commitment of Owen to his part suggested the latter. Very few men would be willing to take a swim in the Thames at this time of year. Also, aside from the ongoing fraud of the director, who was already in the process of being apprehended, there was no evidence of any other crime.

"But there was another detail, one of those trivialities which often proves infinitely important, that kept nagging at me as I leafed through page after page of records."

"That Peters had left unexpectedly?" queried Mycroft.

"Precisely! That Peters, the employee whom Owen had succeeded, had left the bank unexpectedly. I have often expounded upon the importance of imagination to detection, and it was as I was wading through that paperwork and thinking about Peters, that a real possibility began to emerge. What if Peters was coerced or bribed into leaving so that Owen could take his place? It would just be possible if the timing was right, if a word was spoken in the right ear, if there was a director present who was already compromised. This is all simple enough. But why had Owen been planted? What could he have been after? If investigators had been closely watching the bank and building a case against the director, it would have been difficult for Owen to have stolen any money, and recent events seem to indicate a greater sophistication. As I opened yet another manila folder, I had an epiphany. What if it wasn't the actual money or even individual transactions, but about this aggregation of their surrogates, the records and ledgers themselves? One could learn a great deal about people from their financial records: their whereabouts, their travels, their contacts, employers, associations. A criminal or espionage organization could do much with such information. At the moment, I know of no such criminal enterprise that would be up to such a scheme, not since Moriarty fell to his death at the Reichenbach Falls. But Mycroft, I was wondering if perhaps your people had any dealings with the Imperial Bank?"

"Oh, Sherlock, this time you have outdone yourself. Obviously, this is not to leave this room without my consent, but we do have...agents that could possibly be tracked, given this scenario you have constructed. And Adolph Meyer, a particularly slippery German agent, matches Pierpont's description of the eyebrowless, long-mouthed assailant and is known to be in London. I shall see if I can discover his exact whereabouts."

"Excellent. I have already begun a search for Owen and will contact you tomorrow to inform you of its progress."

As we emerged from the Diogenes Club and made our way back into the evening's fog, though it was as yet unknown to me, Holmes's search was already proceeding, as countless street arabs, the neglected children of London, crept from alley to alley and from rooftop to rooftop in the murky, gas-lit gloom, in search of the banker, Owen. Holmes had provided Wiggins, the leader of this ragtag legion, which Holmes had dubbed the "Baker Street Irregulars," with the photograph he had borrowed from the bank and offered a reward to the boy who could find Owen first.

While this unseen manhunt continued, Holmes and I returned to Baker Street so that he could root through the agony columns of recent newspapers in search of some communications between the spies. Though Holmes had frequently been rewarded in the past by such sources, he was destined to be frustrated that night. By the early hours of the morning, he must have given up, for I heard from my chamber the discordant tones of his violin below.

By morning, the fog of acrid tobacco smoke in our sitting room rivaled that of the city without. Refusing breakfast, Holmes paced nervously and continued to consume pipe after pipe of shag. Finally, at a little after ten o'clock, a district messenger arrived with word from Mycroft. Much to Holmes annoyance, he unfortunately had been unable to track down Meyer's whereabouts. But just as the young messenger opened the door to leave the house, a raggedly dressed and dirty adolescent squeezed past him and bounded up the stairs to pound rapidly on our door.

"Ah, Wiggins! I see that for once you have followed my instructions to leave the rest of the lads outside," said Holmes, as he opened the door. "We don't want to upset Mrs Hudson. Now, quickly, have you run our prey to ground?"

"Stinson saw him on his way back to his flat after lunch. He lives at 110 Vine Street in Aldgate, flat number two. He only just told me about it, so Owen should still be there. Stinson posted Buckley to stand watch, just in case, though."

"Excellent, Wiggins! Please give this and my thanks to Stinson and take this for yourself. Also, please go and take this note to Inspector Lestrade at Scotland Yard."

When he had finished writing, he handed the note to Wiggins who bounded back down the stairs with it. At Holmes suggestion, I retrieved my service revolver and we made our way by cab without delay to Aldgate. We stopped just around the corner from Vine Street and walked to a nearby pub to await Lestrade. We didn't have long to wait, and within half an hour, we had brought Lestrade up to speed over a pint. Having agreed upon a course of action, we departed the pub and walked around the corner into Vine Street. Number 110 was a small, but nondescript house in the centre of the block. In the entrance hall, a small, greasy-haired boy was playing cards, but on seeing Holmes, he gathered up the deck and approached us.

"He's still there, Mr Holmes."

"Thank you, Buckley. If you could do just one more thing for me, there's a shilling in it for you. My friends and I are going to quietly go upstairs and stand by the door of number two. Once we are in position, I want you to come upstairs, bang on the door of the flat, and announce that you have a message for a Mr Owen from a Mr Pierpont. Here, take this in case he can see you from within," said Holmes as he handed the eager boy a blank piece of paper and his shilling.

We made our way silently up the stairs. The apartment was to our left on the second floor, and Holmes moved to the left of the door, while Lestrade and I stood to the right with our revolvers drawn. We were no sooner in place than we heard Buckley come bounding up the stairs. He ran over and stopped before the door.

"Delivery! I have a message for a Mr Owen!" he cried as he knocked on the door. A muffled voice responded from within.

"What? You must be mistaken...There's no one here by that name."

"It says it's for Mr Owen of number two from a Mr Pierpont!"

"But that's not..."

Suddenly, there was the sound of a bolt being drawn, and the door cautiously opened. Behind it was the man I had seen identified in the photograph at the bank, Mr Lester Owen. The guns Lestrade and I pointed at him were the first things he saw, and he froze as Holmes stepped into the open.

"Hello, Mr Owen. I am Sherlock Holmes, and these are my friends and colleagues, Dr Watson and Inspector Lestrade. Please be so good as to let us in and keep your hands where we can see them."

Owen backed nervously into the one-room flat and took a seat upon the bed as Holmes motioned for him to do. The suitcase that lay open upon it indicated what he had been doing before our arrival.

"Watson, please keep him covered," Holmes requested as Lestrade cuffed Owen's hands together.

"Now, Mr Owen, we can talk, and indeed, it will do you no good to keep silent. We know about your information gathering at the bank, we know about your passing this information on to the German spy, Adolph Meyer, and we know about your attempt to fake your own death so that you could escape punishment for your treason and perhaps go on to repeat it at another establishment."

"Wait! Treason? I'm not sure how, but you seem to know even more of this matter than I."

"Your contact was a known German agent," interjected Lestrade. "And I'm sure you know the penalty for treason."

"If you can explain to us, it might not go as heavily with you," resumed Holmes.

"But what you say can be used against you," added Lestrade.

"I understand, but truly I am no traitor. He called himself Lang, and I did not know he was a spy…or even German, for that matter. He said he only wanted some occasional information—to find out if an account existed for a particular person, if certain transactions were occurring in certain cities, if certain people were conducting business. He wouldn't tell me why, but he offered me enough money that I hardly cared. Of course, I knew it was unethical, but we never stole anything or tampered with any records. Although, now that you have made this accusation, I can see how such information could have been used. But I swear that, at the time, I didn't know!"

"If you are really still at all loyal to your country, I may be able to furnish you with a chance to prove it. But first, what happened to Peters, the man you replaced at the bank?"

"I was going through a rough patch, having just got the sack from a position at an insurance company that was about to go under, when I met Lang at Nicholson's Pub. As we spoke, he became more familiar with me and said a position was about to open at the Imperial Bank. He said that if I was to apply, he was sure they would find me to be the right man for the job. He winked and promised to make a considerable investment in me in order to insure it. I knew it wasn't all above board, but I would've grasped at anything in my sorry state."

"Why choose such an elaborate method of disappearing?"

"Lang, or Meyer, was one of those types who thought himself clever. He said he had concocted an ingenious way for me to disappear so that I might be able to work for him elsewhere without a hint of suspicion. He asked me if there was someone at work who knew me and whose testimony would never be questioned. Pierpont seemed perfect. I wasn't exactly thrilled with the prospect of diving into the Thames, but I'm a strong swimmer, and it wasn't as awful as I thought it was going to be. In that dense fog, all I had to do was paddle away a short distance. Meyer then helped to lift me out after pretending to chase Pierpont."

"Who was the woman Pierpont had been following?"

"An associate of Meyer's. I only knew her as Helena, and Meyer had instructed her in advance. Meyer would stand outside the bank and watch for my signal. When I saw Pierpont leaving for lunch, I placed a lamp in my office window with a mirror behind it to increase its illumination. Meyer, upon seeing it, would signal Helena so that she could get a head start. She was to lead Pierpont around through the alleys until we would be ready at the docks, exactly twenty minutes after the signal."

"I think that about answers my questions. Now I will offer you a chance to prevent any further damage resulting from this scheme. Are Meyer and his confederate still in London?"

"I know nothing of her, Mr Holmes, but Meyer said I would be able to reach him until tomorrow if an emergency arose."

"And how would you reach him?"

"There is an unoccupied flat two blocks down the street. It is unfurnished save for a table, a lamp, and a mirror. When I wish to meet with him, I go to the flat and give the same signal that I used at the bank. He then comes here, usually between nine and ten in the evening."

"Very good. Lestrade, Watson and I will go give the signal and notify my brother, Mycroft, that we may yet be able to apprehend Meyer. Meet us back here in an hour with some of your men. I want someone in this flat soon after that lamp is lit, regardless of the traditional meeting time."

"I'll have the place surrounded before you return, Holmes."

I happen to have a similar build to Owen's, so just in case Meyer was watching, Holmes thought it best that I go to the flat and give the signal and then meet Holmes and Lestrade back at Owen's apartment. In the meantime, Holmes walked to a nearby post office to send a telegram to Mycroft. By three o'clock, Holmes, Lestrade, and I were together again in Owen's flat, and Lestrade's men were covering the exits of the building and occupying other floors. Even Mycroft Holmes, in an almost unthinkable deviation from his routine, joined us in our vigil. We sat for hours in the little room, Lestrade and Holmes standing on either side of the door, and Mycroft and I sitting along the wall behind the bed, listening carefully to the other tenants going about their business.

Finally, at a little after nine, we heard footsteps slowly ascend the stairs and begin walking along the hallway toward the apart-ment. Lestrade and I drew our guns while Holmes brandished the loaded riding crop that was his weapon of choice. The footsteps halted at our door and before our quarry was able to knock a sec-ond time, Lestrade had pulled the door open. Meyer, however, was already holding a revolver in his hand, and it was pointed squarely at my head as the door swung open. In an instant, the loaded butt of Holmes's crop descended on the villain's wrist with a sharp crack, no doubt fracturing it and releasing his grip upon the pistol. As Meyer howled in pain and frustrated rage, Lestrade pressed the barrel of his gun to the spy's temple.

"Don't move, Meyer, as neither of my friends will hesitate to fire! Lestrade, is he alone?"

"Yes, Holmes. Come along, lads, and help me get this black-guard downstairs!" yelled Lestrade as several detectives descended the stairs to Owen's flat.

As we followed Lestrade and his captive out of the building, Mycroft ruminated, "Excellent work, Sherlock. Even if we have only prevented him from transmitting his most recently obtained information, he will make an excellent trade for any of our operatives who may have been captured as a result of this scheme."

"But what about his mysterious accomplice?" I wondered aloud.

"Yes, she may already be back on the continent," replied Holmes, "but if she isn't, we at least know what she looks like. And you have to admit, we did not do badly for three days's work. Now, I propose we make our way over to Nicholson's for a toast and a bite to eat, while Mycroft decides what we should tell Mr Pierpont."

✗

THE PROBLEM OF THE THREE EDWARDIAN PENNIES

by Peter Cannon

"I confess, Dr Watson," said Mr Arthur Machen, "that I am not altogether an enthusiast for the profession of journalism. Yet as a newspaper reporter I have seen queer things and odd prospects which, otherwise, I should not have seen."

"And I, sir, am not altogether an enthusiast for the profession of medicine," I replied. "Especially now that there is little to distract me from it."

The journalist and I were seated one winter evening in the lounge of the Dog and Duck in High Holborn, where at that period we were in the habit of meeting over a convivial pint or two. Since the retirement of Sherlock Holmes to the country, to live as a hermit among his bees and his books, I had been at a loss for provocative intellectual company and so had welcomed the chance to cultivate the acquaintance of such a character as Arthur Machen. A sometime actor, with a deep and resonant voice, he could converse on a wide and various range of subjects as naturally as Dr Johnson, whom with his stocky build and large head he passably resembled. The author of a handful of stories and novels of an occult or mystical cast, he was convinced that the thinnest of veils separated humanity from some unknown world of wonder, beyond the ken of science.

"In my experience, coincidence figures more often in life than is commonly assumed," the sage continued. "Have I told you the singular tale of Campo Tosto and Burnt Green?"

"You mean the eccentric old Belgian of Italian extraction whose name was practically a translation of the place where he lived; the medieval art collector who shot at intruders with bow and arrow; the late gentleman who left his estate, mostly fifteenth-century Madonnas and altar candlesticks, to his servant bearing the good old English country name of Turk? My dear fellow, how could I forget?"

"As I was saying, Dr Watson, in my experience coincidence figures more often than is commonly assumed. For example, would you believe that the other day I ran into your former associate, Mr Sherlock Holmes?"

"Good heavens! Where?"

"At an inquest."

"On a corpse?"

"No, on a treasure-trove, found on the Suffolk coast."

Not the least of my drinking companion's charms, I was coming to realize, was his robust sense of humour. Holmes was less than a faithful correspondent, and the reporter must have known that I would be keen to hear news of his doings.

"So this was no criminal investigation."

"I am afraid not, though there was a mystery involved, as strange as any I daresay your friend the famed detective encountered in his professional career."

"I am all ears, sir."

"In brief, here was the case." The journalist handed me a cutting from a morning paper dated the previous week on the recovery of a cache of coins, exposed by a storm at sea. That same day, he added, his own editor had despatched him to Liverpool Street, to catch a train bound for Suffolk.

"There was no railway station anywhere near the desolate spot where this incident had occurred. The station where I disembarked from the train was full six miles away from the shore, and the population it served was lodged in an inn and half a dozen cottages. I hired a man and a trap and drove off over a level country in the face of a frosty east wind.

"At last we reached the shore, marked by a cliff, or rather by a bank of sand ten or twelve feet high. On this height local fishermen had been standing a few days earlier, watching the raging storm and the great waves that blew in from the east. Suddenly, one mighty billow had brought down a whole stretch of this sandy cliff. And as the wave washed back, the men of the inner heights noticed something bright and gleaming in the wash of waters. They retrieved what they could, and the learned being called in, pronounced that here were very ancient coins.

"I arrived, it seemed, in the very nick of time. I was shown to a chamber in a martello tower, where men in blue jerseys, supervised by some official personage and observed by a number of curiosity seekers, were busy counting out the coins and sealing them into little packets; to be ready, I suppose, for the Crowner's Quest, on the part of our lord the King.

"And it was an astounding treasure. I am no numismatologist, but to the best of my belief, the earliest coins were dated of the eleventh or twelfth century. The dates went on in a sparse scattering way through the centuries; here a coin of Richard I, then one of Henry III, then one of Edward II; a gap perhaps to Henry VIII; then, a shilling of Elizabeth; and so forth. And then, here was the shock, here the true interest: three pennies of Edward VII.

"Afterwards, as I was leaving the martello tower, I fell into conversation with another unofficial witness who had been equally struck by this anomaly. A tall, lean fellow of about fifty, he explained that he had happened to be in the area, researching local folklore for a monograph he was writing, when news of the find reached him. Since he had walked the six miles from the inn where he was staying, he was glad to accept my offer of a lift.

" 'There are so many questions, sir,' I remarked as the trap set off through the monotonous sand dunes, the bitter wind at least now at our backs. 'What was the queer hoard? How did it come to be gathered together? Who gathered it? How did the great wave discover it? Was it washed from the sea? Or was it washed from the cliff? I confess the problem almost as intolerable as the puzzles of Achilles and the Tortoise and the lying Cretans.'

The problem is indeed a deep one,' the gentleman answered, 'though I imagine more susceptible to solution than any abstract logical paradox.'

" 'You cannot say that here was the collection of a numismatologist, even if you could get over the difficulty of such a collection being hidden in the sandy cliff or cast into the sea; both of them most unlikely places for keeping coins. At any rate, a chap interested in old coins would never think of including Edward VII pennies in his collection.'

"The fellow merely nodded, seemingly absorbed in his own thoughts, and we rode in silence for the remaining miles across that flat, windswept landscape. The little cluster of cottages, with their smoking chimneys, came as a most welcome sight. I declined my companions's invitation to join him for a spot of tea at the inn, as I needed to catch the next train to London.

" 'A pity you have to rush off. I was looking forward to sharing a fire with an audience sure to be sympathetic to my theory behind this mysterious treasure-trove.'

" 'I have a few minutes before my train departs, if you wouldn't mind waiting with me at the station.'

"As we alighted from the trap, I had the definite sense that this tall, lean stranger was having a bit of fun at my expense.

" 'A little way inland on this dreary coast, perhaps under a thorn or an elder tree,' he began once we gained the platform, 'there must be a well. This well was once a holy well, St. Somebody's Well. Those who made small pilgrimages to it and uttered their vows there were accustomed to drop offerings into the water. As time went on, the sanctity became hazy, the name of the patron saint was forgotten; but there was a lingering, decaying belief that there was something different here from the wells of common use. During the recent storm a wave drove in a subterranean channel and, as it were, sucked the bottom out of this well, and bore away, as it washed back to sea, the votive offerings that had been dropped there, even from the days of Coeur de Lion to the days of our present Royal Highness.'

" 'Bravo, sir. Your solution is worthy of Sherlock Holmes himself!'

" 'At your service, though it is but a conjecture, my dear Mr Machen.'

" 'Great Scott! Mr Holmes! This is indeed a surprise, as well as an honor.'

" 'The honor is all mine, sir. It is not every day that I get to meet a London literary man of your stature.'

" 'Why, I should have guessed… But how on earth did you know my name?'

" 'At the inquest the diligence with which you scribbled in your notebook suggested your profession; while your anxiousness to return to the capital, prompted no doubt by a deadline, clinched the matter. As for knowing your name, there I admit I was lucky. When we first spoke I recalled that my friend Dr Watson had mentioned, in a recent letter, gathering at a pub with a journalist whose lively intelligence rivaled my own. This fellow, one Arthur Machen, incidentally reminded him of Dr Johnson. If I may say so, in both your verbal manner and your physical presence, sir, you evoke the great Cham.'

" 'You flatter me, Mr Holmes.'

" 'When you next see Dr Watson, please apologize for my not communicating more often. I promise to write to my Boswell shortly. In the meantime, I am tempted to return to the coast tomorrow, to see if I might uncover some actual evidence of a well to support my conjecture. It might well form the basis of a chapter in my Folklore of East Anglia.' "

"As well he might say," I interrupted. "I cannot help wondering, sir, whether in truth my old friend's deductive powers have gone stale since he retired. His theory of a forgotten holy well is ingenious, I grant, but I shouldn't be astonished if it were to come out that certain Suffolk fishermen had slipped those three Edward VII pennies into the cache of coins, as a jest, before delivering the hoard to the learned. As Occam tells us, the simplest explanation is usually the correct one."

"Come, come, Dr Watson," said Arthur Machen with a laugh. "I think you could do with another cup of the Dog and Duck's own excellent punch. As I recall, this round is on me."

THE CURSE OF EDWIN BOOTH

by Carole Buggé

Every family has its defining tragedy. The night my younger brother John Wilkes clutched a pistol in his hand and dragged himself from the depths of a dingy boarding house to Ford's Theatre, resolved to kill President Lincoln, a blackness descended upon the entire nation. But it was a doubly dark time for our family—we had to contend not only with the loss of a great leader, but the shame of being forever identified with that terrible act.

With the firing of a single bullet, everything changed. We continued on, but our lives had lost their sharpness and splendor. We were fortunate to have stalwart friends who stood by us, and though some blamed the entire family, for the most part the public was sympathetic to us. John Wilkes was the only Booth who identified with the South during the war; the rest of us considered ourselves Northerners.

In the year 1880 all of New York knew of Edwin Booth. I could hardly go into the streets without strangers coming up to me and asking me for an autograph, a handshake, a lock of my hair. My father Junius Brutus Booth was a great Shakespearean actor, and my reputation equaled—some even said surpassed—his renown.

It was also in the spring of that same year I became quite certain someone was trying to kill me.

After performances, I was given to late night roaming, striding the streets of the great city, savoring the sensation of being just another anonymous wanderer ducking in and out of yellow pools of light cast by the gaslights. My rambles took me far abroad, to all manner of neighborhoods, from the grand avenues to the seediest side streets. The more my feet toiled, the more peaceful and still I grew inside, as though my perturbed spirit was soothed by the forward motion of my body.

One night, as I emerged from the theatre, a shot rang out from what appeared to be an empty street. I felt a burning sensation on my neck, and when I clapped my hand to the spot, it came away wet with fresh blood.

As an actor and theatre manager, I had faced many situations which required keeping a cool head, so I did not panic. I stepped quickly back through the stage door. The wound on my neck was superficial, and I was soon able to stop the bleeding. I told no one what had happened; my concern for my own safety was tempered by the realization that I was a public figure, and adverse publicity could be ruinous for my theatre company. When I next emerged I had two husky stage hands on either side of me. I told them that I was feeling faint; they hustled me into a waiting carriage, the driver put the horses into a brisk trot, and I was home within minutes.

This was not the first time I had been fired upon. A year earlier a mentally unbalanced man by the name of Mark Gray had shot at me during a performance. But for some odd reason that night—perhaps somehow sensing what was to come—I stood during a monologue in which I usually remain seated, and the bullet whizzed harmlessly past me. He was immediately arrested, and we were able to finish the performance. My reaction at the time was a kind of giddiness—I had narrowly escaped death, my assailant was quickly put in jail, and all was well.

However, this time my feeling was one of dark terror—so dark, in fact, that I took a step I never would have imagined taking: I put an advertisement in the paper.

Wanted: Professional detective for private employment. Must be discreet, trustworthy. Experience with Pinkerton Agency or similar employment preferred. Possibly dangerous; monetary reward considerable. Only serious applicants need apply. Reply to Post Office Box 28.

The reference to Allan Pinkerton and his excellent agency was bitterly ironic, since he had foiled an assassination attempt on President Lincoln in 1861, only to watch helplessly with the rest of the nation as my brother gunned down the great man a few years later.

I took no one into my confidence save my ancient and faithful Negro servant, Hector, who had been with our family since my boyhood in Maryland. After my father's death, he became my constant attendant and companion; a more competent and considerate man could not be found this side of the Atlantic.

The paper in which I had placed the advertisement had been at the newsstands and book stalls just a few hours when there was a knock upon the front door of the Players Club. I was in the grill room having a late lunch, and as the doorman was also taking a late lunch, I sent Hector to answer it.

The Players Club is a sturdy three-story brownstone on Gramercy Park South I had purchased and remodeled to serve as a meeting place for prominent men of the theatre, as well as other outstanding professionals. (Membership was by invitation only, and our earliest members included Mark Twain, John Drew, and General William Tecumseh Sherman.) The first two floors included a pool room and a small theatre, as well as a grill room and bar on the first floor; I occupied the third floor when I was in New York.

When Hector ushered our visitor into the grill room, I knew at once he was a singular and extraordinary man. I have an actor's instinct for character, and am used to sizing up people quickly. His eyes were dark—so dark that they appeared black in the dim light, reminding me of the Indians I had known in my youthful days in California. He was taller than average; I would have guessed well over six feet—but then many men appear tall to me, as I am only five foot seven in my stocking feet. The Booth family may have had its share of talent, but it did not breed giants.

His face and figure were long and lean; I was reminded of Cassius in Julius Caesar (which we were doing in repertory with Hamlet), whom Shakespeare describes as having "a lean and hungry look." (Sadly, our current Cassius, Geoff Simmons, was overly fond of sausages and porter, and was anything but lean—in his green toga, he rather suggested a fat garden slug wrapped in a leaf.)

My visitor's expression was one of keen interest and curiosity. I had the impression nothing much escaped those deep-set eyes; he seemed to take in everything around him at a glance. Though he could not have been older than thirty, something in his manner told me here was someone I could trust. He wore a simple but expensive frock coat and vest, with perfectly pressed trousers and shining black boots.

"How do you do, Mr. Booth?" he said.

As an actor, I have a highly developed ear for voices; I realized at once his educated and refined accent was the product of an upper-class British background. I wondered what business he had with me.

"I have arrived in answer to your advertisement," he continued, evidently in response to my bemused expression.

"But the advertisement gave no address—only an anonymous post office box."

He waved away my objections as if they were an annoying insect.

"A mere formality—I assure you it was not difficult to discover who you were."

I stared at him. "How on earth did you—"

"That you were well off was evident from the suggestion of considerable monetary reward."

As a child, I had suffered from a stutter, which had conquered years ago. To my surprise, I felt it beginning to return now.

"Yes, b-but—"

"That you were well known was evident from the phrase regarding discretion."

"But how d-did you know it was me—this city is full of well-known people!"

"It was a simple matter to follow this gentleman from the post office," he said, indicating Hector, who had just brought me half a dozen letters on a silver tray. "I had my eye on Box number twenty-eight, and when he looked inside for the replies, I knew he would lead me to you. I had only to follow him here."

I felt the tension of the past twenty-four hours begin drain away from my shoulders.

"Oh, so it was a bit of detective work after all! All you had to do was wait patiently at the post office for him to turn up, and then follow him. So all those deductions about my being well-known and wealthy were just—"

"Oh, no—I had already deduced those facts before seeing your servant."

"I see."

"So when I followed him here, I was quite certain I had the right man."

I looked around the grill room. The bar-tender was busily polishing glasses, and several actors were congregated in the back of the room, laughing and talking among themselves. I thought privacy was called for, so I summoned Hector, who stepped soundlessly into the room. Though well into his seventies, his elegant posture and unlined face gave Hector the appearance of a much younger man. He was tall and dignified, with deep brown skin as lustrous as polished mahogany. You would never guess his age by looking at his smooth skin stretched taut across high cheekbones. Only his hands, worn with years of domestic service, betrayed his age.

"Hector, would you show my visitor up to the second floor lounge?" I said. "And bring us up a bottle of brandy and two glasses, please."

There was a small, cozy second floor room on the east side of the building, mostly used for playing cards, which was unlikely to be occupied in the middle of the afternoon.

"Yessir," said Hector, bowing slightly, the gold of the lamplight reflecting on his shiny bald head. The bow was for our visitor's sake; Hector never observed such formalities when it was just the two of us.

I settled my tab in the grill room and headed up the stairs after them—I always insisted on paying for my meals, even though I owned the building. My visitor was seated comfortably in the lounge, his long body folded into a burgundy leather arm chair.

"I am perhaps not what you expected," he commented as I took the chair opposite him.

"I must admit I was expected a somewhat rougher type of man."

"Rest assured that I am the man you seek," he replied smoothly.

"Brandy?" I asked, myself a sifter of the golden liquid.

"It is perhaps a bit early for brandy," he remarked, removing his gloves. His hands were long, with tapered fingers.

"Tea, then?" I said. "Coffee?"

"Coffee, I think," he replied. "Thank you."

"Do they still drink much coffee in London?" I asked.

He smiled. "It is becoming increasingly popular, though still not as widely consumed as tea. You must give us our idiosyncrasies; after all, we are English. And may I compliment you on your ear for accents, by the way; you are quite correct in surmising that I have spent time in London."

I felt my face warm at his words; even though he was the younger man by at least ten years, I felt like a puppy being praised by his master.

"Now then," I said, "Mr.—?"

"My name is Holmes—Sherlock Holmes."

"Holmes, is it? What a curious thing, indeed."

"What is curious?"

"My dear first wife Mary's maternal family name was Holmes."

"Her mother, then, was a Holmes?"

"Yes."

"It is not an uncommon name."

"True…this will sound hopelessly superstitious, but we actors are superstitious folk, so forgive me. But it feels almost as if your coming here was an act of providence—as if my dear Mary were somehow looking after me from beyond the grave."

"I am very sorry to hear your wife has passed away."

"Thank you."

"And yet you are remarried," he commented, indicating the ring on my left hand.

"Yes—though my current wife has quite lost her wits, poor thing. Her name is Mary, also, and she now lives with her parents, who have never cared much for me. She hardly knows who I am— or who anyone is, for that matter." I sighed deeply. "But on to the matter at hand," I said, doing my best to shake off my black mood.

"Yes indeed," he replied. "Now, then, what can I do for you?"

I realized at that moment he had been interviewing me, rather than the other way around, and now was operating under the assumption that the job was his. I felt a bit put out by this, and wanted to protest, but instead I blurted out, "I'm afraid someone is trying to kill me."

He nodded, as if completely unsurprised by this. "Yes, I thought as much."

"How could you possibly know that?"

"You have entirely neglected to put on a cravat. You are either a man in danger or a man newly in love. As you have evidently been married for some time, I deduce the former rather than the latter."

"You have experience in these matters, then, Mr. Holmes?"

"I can provide references, should you require them."

"Somehow I don't think that will be necessary," I replied.

"Good; time is of the essence. Now then, please tell me everything, being careful to omit no detail."

He was the kind of man who immediately inspires confidence in others; the mere fact of his presence was strangely calming.

"Well, the first incident seemed innocent enough at the time: a hanging flat in the theatre swung down during a performance, and I ducked just in time to prevent being decapitated."

"I see. Was the cause of the accident ever determined?"

"It seems someone had forgotten to tie up the rope holding it in place—or tied it so loosely that it came undone. No one came forward to confess to having tied the rope badly."

Holmes nodded gravely. "And the second incident?"

"A trap door on the stage collapsed during rehearsal. When I stepped on it, it gave way and I nearly fell twenty feet into the building's basement."

"And did you ascertain the reason for this odd occurrence?"

"The bolts holding the hinges on had been removed, so that when I stepped on it, the entire thing gave way. Fortunately, an alert stage hand who happened to be standing next to me grabbed my arm and prevented me from falling. I am not an alarmist, Mr. Holmes, but it quite unnerved me."

Holmes leaned back in his chair and placed his long fingers together.

"Who else knows about this?"

"Well, everyone saw the incidents take place, so my entire company, I suppose."

"Was any innocent explanation for this possible?"

"It just so happened that some workmen had been installing some new floorboards the day before, so everyone blamed them. But something felt off to me."

"Have you told anyone else about your suspicions?"

"No. I kept it to myself—except for the anonymous advertisement in the paper which you answered."

He smiled grimly. "That is good—very good. Continue to keep your own counsel. It is essential we preserve as much secrecy as possible."

"I agree."

"Good." He leaned forward to sip his coffee, the lamplight shining on his thick black hair, which he wore combed back from his high forehead. "And the third incident?"

"How do you know there was a third?"

"My dear Mr. Booth, as you yourself stated, you are not an alarmist. The first two incidents, while disturbing, are by no means conclusive evidence of intent to harm you. And yet you went so far as to place an advertisement in the paper; I therefore assume there was a third incident."

"You're quite right, Mr. Holmes—there was a third incident." I paused and took a sip of brandy, which burned my throat with a comforting familiarity. "A few days ago someone tried to shoot me."

Holmes raised a single eyebrow. "I assume you failed to get a look at your assailant?"

"I'm afraid I didn't see him at all. It was dark, and—"

He waved a long hand impatiently. "Tell me what happened. Try to omit nothing in your account."

"I had just finished a performance, and I was leaving the theatre after lingering to talk to the stage manager about the following day's rehearsal. As I turned the corner out into the street from the alley leading to the stage door, I heard the report of a gun."

"You are quiet certain it was a gunshot?"

I took a deep breath; I was not anxious to dwell on the sound of gunshots in theatres.

"Yes. I heard a whistling in my ear, then felt a burning sensation on the side of my neck." I opened my collar and showed him the thin red slash across my neck. Holmes examined it, frowning, then leaned back in his chair.

"You didn't by any chance recover the bullet in question?"

I shook my head. "I was too shaken to even think to look for it."

"And your assailant?"

"I saw no one. That corner is very dark late at night, and the lights in front of the theatre had been turned off."

"I see. Were there any other people about?"

"No; as I said, it was quite late by then. The street looked deserted."

"Your fears seem to be quite justified, Mr. Booth—not only is someone trying to kill you, but I am very much afraid it may be someone known to you—perhaps even a member of your company."

He now accepted my offer of a glass of brandy, and I poured myself some more as well, my hand shaking a little as I grasped the crystal decanter. Alcohol is my only true vice, as it was my father's before me. I have struggled all my life to control my drinking, but now I might be forgiven for indulging in a glass of brandy.

Holmes must have read my mind, for he lifted his glass and said softly, "Yes, Mr. Booth, I do think you might have a second glass of brandy, under the circumstances."

I stared at him. "How could you—?"

He smiled. "The cross hatching of veins across the bridge of your nose, the unusual ruddiness of your cheeks, in spite of your naturally sallow complexion, the slight tremor in your hands; the signs are not hard to miss. You struggle, as many good men do, with an urge toward excessive alcohol consumption. I would even venture to guess that it runs in your family; these things often do. Like your gift for acting—perhaps it is in your blood, as they say."

I nodded, reddening. "Is there anything you do not know, Mr. Holmes?"

Holmes took a sip from his glass. "Most people observe, but they do not see. I have made it my business to not only see, but more importantly, to conclude. For instance, for some years now I have made a study of violent crime, garnered from the newspaper reports of several countries, including yours. I have concluded that the majority of violent crimes are perpetrated not upon strangers by hardened criminals, as today's lurid newspaper reports might have you believe—but occur much more often between people who know each other. Wives poison husbands, children murder their parents, nephews steal from their rich aunt and uncles, and so on."

"What a charming picture you paint of humanity, Mr. Holmes."

"My low opinion of humanity is not the issue here, Mr. Booth. You are in danger; that is my sole concern at present."

"What do you propose I do? I cannot simply refuse to go out in public—I am an actor, for god's sake!"

"What about using an understudy? Surely you must—"

I rose and paced the room distractedly. "If I put on an understudy in my place, people will demand their money back. I say this in all humility, Mr. Holmes: people come to the theatre to see me as Hamlet, as Brutus, as Iago. They do not come to see an understudy."

"I quite understand. But is not disappointing your public worth paying for with your life?"

"It is not that simple, Mr. Holmes. Scores of people depend upon me for their livelihood. I can't cancel performances indefinitely—the theatre and its employees would lose thousands of dollars every night."

Holmes cocked his head to one side and regarded me, his dark eyes seeming to burrow into my very soul. "I can see that you are a man of high principles and courage, Mr. Booth. The vast majority of humanity lives quiet lives with no thought of desperate deeds. If I believed in such things, I would say that your family was cursed."

I laughed bitterly. "You are not the first to suggest it."

I gazed out of the window, where cold gusts whipped the tree branches along Gramercy Park. It was May, but a chill wind had overtaken the city in the last few days. People drew their cloaks close around them as dried leaves scattered by the gusts circled them like miniature tornadoes, bent on knocking them from their feet. I looked back at Holmes, who sat still as a Sphinx, his long fingertips pressed together.

An idea suddenly seized me.

"Have you done any acting, Mr. Holmes?"

"As a matter of fact, I have."

"I knew it! You can always tell a man who has been upon the stage—the way he uses his voice, the way he holds himself. I have recently lost my Horatio. I was about to hold auditions for the role, but now it occurs to me—have you ever done Shakespeare?"

"I confess I have, a little."

"Would you be so kind as to take over the role?"

He paused for a moment. "I think I perceive what you have in mind. Being a member of the cast would give me unparalleled access to the people who surround you professionally."

"Exactly! Well—what do you say? I'll pay you a salary of twenty dollars a week—in addition to your fee, of course."

He smiled, softening the angular planes of his long face, like the sun breaking through the clouds on a gloomy day.

"Why not? I don't see what we have to lose, and we may have much to gain."

"Capital! I shall introduce you to our stage manager tonight at rehearsal. Where are you staying in New York?"

"At the Hotel Washington."

"You must stay here as my guest—there is a spare bedroom on the third floor, just down the hall from my own. I will see that Hector lays out all the necessary items for your comfort."

"Thank you. That will enable me to watch out for your safety more effectively."

"And now, if you don't mind, I think I shall perhaps try to catch a few hours's sleep, as it promises to be a long evening."

"Certainly."

"Now that you are here, Mr. Holmes, I feel a much greater sense of ease."

"Let us hope that your confidence in me is not misplaced. I will do what I can to earn it," he said, lighting his pipe.

"I have no doubt of that," I said, shaking his hand heartily. "Until tonight, then."

I went upstairs and got into bed; however, I could not sleep. Why would someone in my own company want to kill me? Including stage hands, actors and theatre staff, the list of suspects numbered well over sixty—for our current production alone. I must have fallen into a fitful sleep, because I dreamed that my father was standing in the corner of my room, his face sad and mournful. He was dressed in one of his Shakespearean costumes—in the dim light it appeared to be from a production of Hamlet. I tried to speak to him, but no words would come. He raised an arm toward me, as though he wished to beckon me to him—or perhaps it was in warning; I couldn't tell.

Then the chimes on the grandfather clock in the hall struck five, and a moment later Hector appeared at the door with a cup of coffee. I had the odd sensation that I had not really been asleep when the clock chimed; however, my father had vanished. The only explanation I could imagine was that I was indeed asleep and dreaming of him; I could not bring myself to believe that he had visited me from beyond the grave.

Finishing my coffee quickly, I went downstairs to find Holmes waiting with his overcoat on his arm; we walked briskly to the theatre, which was on Union Square, about half a mile from the Players.

When we arrived, I introduced Holmes to the assembled company. I made up a story about knowing him from my youthful days in California, and no one challenged it. In fact, everyone appeared quite pleased and relieved that we had a new Horatio so soon—except for Geoffrey Simmons, our Polonius, who frowned and pulled at his beard. Geoffrey was an odd fellow—a fine actor, but a strange man. He was short and round, so corpulent that he appeared almost a wide as he was tall. His skin was pink and smooth as a baby's, and with his small, bright blue eyes and mane of white hair, he rather resembled a cherubic Santa Claus. However, he was moody and private, and did not socialize much with the rest of the company; no one could claim to know him very well But he was a great favorite with audiences; his Polonius was both a comical bumbler and an oddly touching father figure to Laertes and Ophelia.

The rehearsal went smoothly; Holmes was an even better Horatio than I had imagined—noble, resolute and sensitive, all the qualities the character should have. He also possessed a darkness which contrasted wonderfully with the upright, steadfast Horatio. He was very effective in his closing speech at the end of the play. Several of the actors congratulated him on it—but Geoff Simmons continued to scowl and pull at his beard.

However, our Laertes, young Nate Carlisle, seemed much taken with him. He watched Holmes with great interest during his scenes, and made it a point of talking to him during breaks. Nate was a lively, nervous young man with golden curls and intense, deep-set eyes of the palest blue. His Laertes was fiery and passionate, and he was an excellent swordsman, equally skilled with the epée and the rapier. I am no mean swordsman myself, but the final duel scene with him was a challenge that kept me on my toes. I had never acted with him before; he had been recommended to me by another theatre manager who had seen his work in Savannah.

He reminded me of my former self—energetic, eager and athletic, full of desire to light the world on fire. By the time rehearsals began he had his lines completely memorized. I watched him during rehearsals somewhat wistfully, knowing that those days were behind me, and that he would be in my position years from now, watching some young actor strut and fret his own hour upon the stage, caught up in the excitement of his own vitality.

But though age has much to tell youth, remembering what it was to be young, youth has little interest in listening, because it does not believe it will ever be old. I knew that one day he would look back, as I have, and wonder where it had all gone—the promise, the adventure, the glamour of a life just beginning, a career on the verge of glory. The sweetest moment of all is the one just before the doing—the breath taken before the fulfillment of a long-sought dream. The savoring afterward is always tinged with sadness, with a bitter aftertaste, and is never as sweet.

Nate stood in the wings, conversing with Holmes, his face eager and flushed with the excitement of youth. "Have you acted in London?"

"Only at university, when I was in school—and not very much; I was more interested in other things," Holmes replied.

"I would love to go to England—I want to see how the English do Shakespeare!" Nate exclaimed as Geoff Simmons sauntered up to them.

"It's highly overrated, my boy," Simmons remarked, never taking his eyes off Holmes.

"I quite agree," Holmes replied, turning a level gaze upon Simmons. "Your Polonius is as good as any I've seen in England."

Simmons was utterly flustered by this, and before he could respond, the bell rang to resume rehearsal.

To my distress, I was finding it difficult to concentrate on the play. I was now in the uncomfortable position of watching everyone around me, studying them and wondering what grudge they might possibly hold against me, what the content of our last exchange was, had I ever slighted them in the past, and so on.

During the break Holmes and I sat in my dressing room talking quietly, and Holmes remarked that we had better keep an eye on Simmons.

"Do you know him from elsewhere?"

"I have never laid on him before," Holmes replied calmly, lighting a cheroot cigar. He seemed to smoke as much as I did—my doctor had warned me about it, but I found it even more difficult to give up than alcohol.

"He doesn't appear to have taken a shine to you," I observed.

"Yes, I noticed that."

I rose from my chair and begin to pace the dressing room. It was a nervous habit inherited from my father, who would often pace when he was ill at ease. I had spent my childhood years following him from town to town, trying to soothe his restless spirit with my banjo playing or storytelling—anything to keep him away from the bottle. Most people regarded him as the greatest American actor of his generation, but even as a young boy I saw that the gift of genius could extract a terrible price.

"Well, Holmes, have you seen anyone else you suspect?"

He shook his head. "It is early yet. Is there anyone who would benefit monetarily from your death?"

"I am worth much more alive; a great many people depend upon me for their livelihood."

He blew a smoke ring into the air above his head; it curled and dissipated into a thin grey mist. "If we rule out money as an explanation, then we are left with more personal motives."

"But who would hate me so much they want to kill me?"

"Oh, it is not necessary that they should hate you personally in order to want to kill you—only that they hate someone or something."

"What do you mean?"

He ran a finger through the faint ring of face powder on the make-up table and gazed at the clutter of cards, dried flowers and notes from well-wishers pasted upon the mirror that adorn every actor's dressing room.

"The mind is a curious thing. Once a diseased thought has taken hold, the symptoms may present in a variety of ways. In that respect it is not unlike the body, actually, in which the same disease may present with radically different symptoms in different people."

"That's true," I said. "When my brother John and I got chicken pox as children, all I had were a few spots and a mild fever, whereas Johnny nearly died...." I fell into silence, suddenly struck by the disturbing thought that it might have been better for the world if he had died.

"Exactly," Holmes replied. "And there are even more bizarre cases than that in the medical literature—which is why diagnosis of disease is so much more art than science. Likewise, the diagnosis of crime has its challenges—in this case, several things present themselves to me. Firstly, the would-be killer is very patient. Secondly, he or she is equally determined. That would most probably rule out a crime of passion—though not necessarily. Are there any ladies in your company especially smitten with you?"

I sighed. "Unfortunately, yes." (Some have described me as handsome; I do not agree. It is true that I have my father's dark eyes—critics are fond of using such words as "luminous" and "lustrous" to describe them—but I think my nose is too prominent and my lips too thin to rank me as truly handsome. I would reserve that description for my brother John, whose high forehead, strong jaw, and noble profile made him a great favorite with the ladies.)

"Do you have a particular admirer in mind?" Holmes inquired.

I sighed again. "Her name is Kitty, and she is a perfectly nice young women, though not much of an actress, I'm afraid. I also suspect that her admiration is not for my person so much as my position, to be honest."

Just then there was rapid, lively knock on the door, and as if responding to a cue, Kitty's voice sounded in the hallway.

"Edwin!" she sang out in her high, bell-like voice. "May I come in?"

"That's her now," I whispered to Holmes.

He beckoned me to open the door.

Kitty was standing in the hall, dressed as a lady in waiting in the Danish court. She dearly wanted to play the part of the doomed Ophelia, but she settled for a non-speaking role instead. It pleased the gentlemen of New York when I sprinkled the stage with comely young woman, and I had no objection to bringing in more audience members, even if they were not there to admire Shakespeare's verse.

"Hello!" Kitty said brightly. Her blond hair bounced in tight ringlets around her face, and her blue eyes were cheerful as spring daisies. "Oh," she said, peering around my shoulder to spot Holmes. "I'm sorry—I didn't realize you had company!"

"Not at all," I said. "Please come in."

"Hello, Mr. Helms," Kitty said.

"Holmes," I corrected.

"Yes, yes—I am sorry, Mr. Holmes!" Kitty corrected herself, blushing prettily.

"You remember Kitty," I said to Holmes. "She plays a lady-in-waiting."

"Of course," he said graciously. "Come in, please."

She gave a little curtsy in response; she came from the slums of the Lower East Side, and was forever at pains to behave like a lady. She entered the room, her fluffy white terrier Prince trailing behind her, his sharp little eyes just visible under the shaggy fur on his head. When he saw Holmes, he gave a high, piercing bark, wagging his stub of a tail.

"Stop it, Prince!" Kitty cried, picking him up and cradling him in her plump white arms.

"Your dog does not appear to like me," Holmes commented.

"Oh, no—he does!" Kitty protested. "He only barks at people he likes."

"Curious," said Holmes. "He wouldn't be much use as a watchdog."

Kitty erupted in peals of silvery laughter. "He's not a watchdog, silly! Did you hear that, Princey? Mr. Holmes thinks you're a watchdog."

She hugged the dog close to her lilac-scented bosom and fluttered her blond eyelashes at us. I mused that she would be more attractive if she weren't so overplaying her hand; as for Holmes, he seemed immune to her charms.

"What can I do for you, Kitty?" I said.

"I was just wondering if it might be a good idea to have more of the members of the court onstage for the final scene," she said, putting the dog back down and twirling a lock of golden hair between her dainty fingers. "It would heighten the tension to have more spectators onstage."

I smiled. Kitty was always anxious to spend more time onstage.

"You may be right," I replied, and her already pink cheeks reddened even more.

"Thank you for the idea," I continued, ushering her to the door.

"You're welcome. Good-bye," she called to Holmes. "Welcome to the company!"

"Thank you very much," he replied. Then, with a rustle of skirts and a flash of yellow hair, she turned, leaving behind a trail of lilac perfume, her little dog trotting obediently after her.

"A very cheerful young woman," Holmes remarked dryly when she had gone. "And a very ambitious one."

I stared at him. "You don't suspect—"

He smiled grimly. "My dear Booth, I suspect everyone."

"But surely—" I began, reddening.

"Your gallant attitude toward the fairer sex does you credit, but one of the most charming women I ever knew drowned all three of her children in a bathtub."

I shuddered.

"Really, Holmes, I would not care to have your perspective on humanity."

"If one wants to engage in solving crime, one must not shy away from the truth."

I was just about to turn my attention to a platter of cold roast beef that had been delivered to my dressing room when the bell rang to resume rehearsal. As the manager of the company as well as its star, I tried never to be late to rehearsal. Disappointed, I gazed longingly at the beef as we hurried off to the stage.

As we approached the famous scene with the gravediggers, I realized I had left Yorick's skull in my dressing room. I hurried back to retrieve it, hoping secretly to grab a piece of roast beef before returning.

The door was ajar, and when I opened it, I saw Kitty's little dog Prince lying on the floor. He was unnaturally still, and I feared the worst. I knelt beside him; he did not appear to be breathing. I felt for a pulse but could find none. I noticed some white foam clinging to the corner of his mouth. I also saw that a chunk of meat had been bitten from the joint of roast beef on the table.

My head began to spin and my knees suddenly went weak. I realized immediately what had happened: the poisoned meat was meant for me. I took several deep breaths in an attempt to steady my nerves. I leaned against the dressing room wall and ran a hand across my clammy forehead; I had broken out into a cold sweat.

There was a quick, light knock at the door. I hesitated for a moment.

"Who is it?"

"Holmes."

Relief flooded my veins, and I opened the door to admit him to the room. He took one look at the poor dog and grasped the situation immediately.

"Dear me," he said, frowning. "This is very bad indeed."

"What should we do?"

"We must remove the dog from here immediately—the killer must not know we are onto him."

"What about that?" I asked, indicating the joint of beef.

"If anyone asks you about it, say you were not hungry and intend to dine tonight at your club."

"Poor Kitty," I said as we lifted the small, lifeless body.

"Yes; it will go hard with her when she discovers him in her dressing room."

"But shouldn't we tell her—"

Holmes shook his head. "It is most regrettable, but also vital that the dog appears to have died of natural causes."

We took the poor creature down the hall to the dressing room Kitty shared with the other ladies in waiting, and left him next to her chair. I felt my throat thicken as we closed the door behind us, and my forehead burned with shame at the ruse we were perpetrating on poor Kitty. I understood Holmes's reasoning, but it did not sit well with me.

"And now?" I said.

"Now we return to rehearsal as though nothing happened."

And so we did. I made some excuse for having been detained for so long, something about being approached by the theatre owner for this month's rent. That went over without a murmur of suspicion; several of the company members nodded in sympathy when I made a disparaging remark about the greed of theatre owners.

But all the while I was on the lookout for any unusual or suspicious behavior—a sideways glance here, a shifting of the eyes there. However, I saw none. Perhaps this was to be expected, I reflected bitterly; after all, I was surrounded by actors, who spend their entire lives dissembling; what could be more natural for a trained actor than to play the role of the innocent, even if he is guilty?

We had just begun Act II when a bloodcurdling wail came from the direction of the dressing rooms. Everyone stopped what they were doing and listened, horrified. It was a woman's voice, and it was a chilling sound that made my skin prick out all over in goose bumps.

I knew, of course, only too well who it was, and why she was crying. Moments later, one of the other young actresses, Carolyn Maloney, rushed into the room, tears streaming down her face.

"It's Kitty!" she wailed. "Her poor little Prince is dead!"

Moments later Kitty appeared, carrying the inert body of her pet dog, her pretty face swollen from crying. I admit my own eyes did not remain entirely dry—the sight was so piteous that I doubt any of us remained unmoved by it.

Kitty was petted and hugged and made much fuss over, but she was inconsolable. No one was more solicitous than young Nate Carlisle, who took her hand in his, and with a trembling voice, expressed his sincere regret. When Kitty wouldn't stop crying, he looked beseechingly at the rest of us.

"You can always get another dog," he suggested hopefully.

"I don't want another dog!" she wailed. "I want my Princey!"

Poor Nate looked miserable, as if he was about to cry himself, and I decided to save him by calling everyone back to rehearsal. It would have been nice to take the rest of the day off, but we were scheduled to open in a week.

Kitty struggled bravely through rehearsal, but it was clear that the death of her beloved dog had devastated her. The shock of grief was stamped on her face—her lower lip trembled during the Queen's speech about Ophelia's death, and she shed real tears during my death scene at the end of the play. If she were only able to summon up such real emotion consistently onstage, she would have been a more successful actress.

After rehearsal, I was waiting in the lobby for Holmes to join me when I saw Joe Jefferson hurrying toward me. He was a tall, lanky gentleman with thin lips, serious dark eyes and a severe face—yet his nature was anything but severe. He came from a theatrical family, as I did, and was one of the leading comedians—perhaps the leading one—of his generation. I had known him since my days in California. He had agreed to play the small but key role of the

First Gravedigger in our production. It was a role he had played many times before, and he was always an audience favorite. The repartee between Hamlet and the Gravedigger is some of Shakespeare's wittiest, one mark of his genius being his ability to relieve the mounting tension of the tragedy with this brief comic scene.

"I say, wait up for a moment!" Jefferson panted, running after me on spindly, stork-like legs. A long black greatcoat hung off his lean, slightly bowed back, and with his coarse black hair and piercing dark eyes, he reminded me of a bird of prey—a crow, perhaps, or a raven.

"Edmund, my boy," he said, catching up with me, "I have something for you." It was one of his little jokes to call me Edmund, which was the name of the evil bastard son in King Lear.

He fished a slip of paper from his pocket and thrust it at me. "Geoff Simmons gave this to me to give to you. You were busy talking with the costume mistress, and he said he was late for an appointment."

"Very well—thank you, Joseph," I replied, slipping the note into my pocket.

"Don't mention it." He began to leave, then turned back to me, his black eyebrows furrowed. "I say, old man, is everything all right?"

"Yes, perfectly—why do you ask?"

"It's just that you look a bit—distracted, I suppose." He leaned closer to me, and I could see the yellow in his eyes. "I say, it's not your wife, is it? Taken a turn for the worse, has she?"

It was Joe Jefferson who had first introduced me to Mary Devlin, my beloved first wife, and I always thought he found my current wife a poor substitute.

"No, no—she's much the same," I answered.

"Poor thing," he clucked, his eyes crinkling sympathetically. "Madness runs in that family," he added with a conspiratorial nod.

"Well, I must be off," I said, buttoning my coat.

Still he lingered, and I began to feel irritated that he would not take a hint and leave.

"That fellow playing Horatio—what's his name?" he said, clearing his throat loudly.

"Uh—Holmes," I replied.

"Yes, Holmes—he's quite good, isn't he?"

"Yes, he is."

"Where did you say you knew him from?"

"California."

He frowned. "I don't remember him in California."

"He showed up after you left."

"It's odd that your father never mentioned him."

My early years in California were spent following my famous father around from town to town, trying to keep him from indulging one of his notorious drinking sprees.

"My poor father's memory was rather affected by his drinking, I'm afraid," I replied with a heavy sigh.

But even the best actor cannot always fool another actor—as with confidence men, we know the tricks of the trade. Jefferson peered at me intently for a moment, looking as though he was about to speak, then shrugged his shoulders and shoved his bony hands deep inside his coat pockets.

"Well, well, do take care, won't you?" he said.

"Yes," I replied, thinking his comment somewhat odd.

"Right, then, old man—see you tomorrow."

With that he loped off into the night, his great coat flapping around his ankles like the wings of a giant black bird.

As I stood watching him, I was suddenly aware that someone was behind me. I turned to see Holmes standing there silently, arms folded, looking after Jefferson.

"Curious man," he remarked.

"How do you mean?" I was both fascinated and irritated with Holmes's ability to pluck observations out of thin air.

"What are your conclusions regarding Mr. Jefferson?" I inquired.

"Oh, nothing much," he answered airily, "other than he owns a Springer spaniel of advanced years, is overly fond of coffee, and is quite the amateur gardener. He is quite keen on roses in particular, I should think."

I stared at him.

"Really, Holmes, how on earth—?"

"Do not distress yourself, my dear Booth. That he owns a dog is evident from the short, curly hairs clinging to his trousers. That it is a medium-sized dog is evident from the fact that the hairs are to found only as far up as his knees. As the hairs and both black and grey and curly, the most obvious choice would be a spaniel, probably a Springer, which is a very popular breed just now."

"But the age of the dog—"

He smiled. "There I confess I was surmising. A man his age does not get a young dog—in fact, if he has a dog at all, it is likely to be as advanced in a dog's years as he is. That and a preponderance of the grey hairs led to my conclusion."

"And the rest of your conclusions? The coffee drinking, for example?"

"One of the first things I noticed was the color of his teeth—and nothing except tobacco can stain the teeth quite that shade of grey. However, as he has not a whiff of smoke about his clothing or his person, I discounted that conclusion and surmised that he is overly fond of coffee."

"And the gardening?"

"Again, simple observation. He is impeccably groomed, and yet his fingernails are ragged and somewhat dirty. That and the ruddy glow of his cheeks leads me to believe he spends time among his flowers—and the scratches on his hands lead me to the conclusion that his particularly fond of roses, which, as poets have oft noted, are not without their thorns. Are you satisfied now?"

"Oh, very well!" I said, sounding a bit exasperated, which was not my intent, but I couldn't help myself. "I'm satisfied, but you have to admit it's a bit—well, irritating."

He smiled. "Perhaps. But just as a man who wishes to improve his bodily strength must do his exercises, so I must exercise my brain. May I ask what you were conversing about just now?"

"He had a note to give me from Geoff Simmons."

"May I inquire what was in it?"

"I haven't read it yet," I said, fishing it out of my pocket. I glanced at it quickly—it was written on the back of one of our programs for Hamlet. I handed it to Holmes, who read it aloud.

"'My dear Edwin, would you kindly meet me tomorrow after rehearsal in the grill room of the Players? I may have something of import to tell you. Geoff Simmons.'"

"What do you make of it?" I asked.

"It's very curious," he murmured, handing it back to me. "Observe the wording: I may have something of import to tell you—it suggests that he does not yet know whether he will or not."

"Yes, I noticed that."

"Furthermore, it is written hurriedly, on the back of a program—as though he did not plan to write it, and just grabbed whatever was to hand at the time."

"Yes, I see what you mean."

"Also, why not request a meeting with you tonight instead of tomorrow?"

"Presumably because of a prior appointment today."

"Indeed. The whole thing is very mysterious, and I don't like it."

We left the theatre, heading northwest toward the Players, starting up Fifth Avenue, before winding west through side streets, past stalls of booksellers and greengrocers. We walked for a while in silence, breathing in the early spring air; the cold snap of the previous week had lifted, and the air was suddenly heavy with the smell of cherry blossoms.

The area around Union Square had become one of the most fashionable in New York, and the outdoor cafés were beginning to fill up. Ladies perched daintily upon narrow café chairs, wobbly on wrought iron legs, festooned in finery and an astounding array of pastels, their matching parasols and lap dogs at their feet. Heading west, we wandered uptown through the gaily decorated theatre district as carriages careened past us, bouncing briskly down Broadway.

"From now on you must only eat food which has been prepared by people you can trust," said Holmes. "Having failed at poisoning once, your assailant will not be prevented from trying again."

"At least now we can eliminate Kitty as a suspect," I observed gloomily.

"Not so, I'm afraid. Just because the plan backfired and her dog ate the poisoned meat by accident, we cannot eliminate her."

"But she was so distraught—"

"My dear Booth, that proves nothing. Her tears would have been just as real if the dog had eaten beef she herself had poisoned; in fact, the bitter irony of having been responsible for her dog's death might have lent even more force to her grief. I might also point out that poison is a traditionally feminine method of killing—"

"All right, Holmes; I take your point," I interrupted moodily. I was beginning to find the whole experience exhausting, and longed to crawl into bed, pull the covers over my head, and be done with the whole wretched affair.

But Holmes was relentless.

"Stealth has now become increasingly important to your assailant. The unsuccessful shooting was a setback—we can at least be grateful for that."

I did not respond; I found it difficult to be grateful for anything, knowing now that any meal I ate could very well be my last.

"He is becoming bolder, which we must use to our advantage, and try to flush him out without his knowledge, and spring a trap on him when he least expects it."

It was late when we arrived at the Players, and the grill room was about to close. However, an exception was usually made for me; I had access to the kitchen around the clock. We ordered lamb chops and roast potatoes, and though I normally am very fond of lamb, I didn't have much appetite. I was silent all throughout dinner, and only when Hector brought us our coffee and brandy in front of the fire did I finally give voice to the thoughts I had been nursing all night.

"I was born with a caul over my head," I began slowly, "and I always attributed to it any luck or success I have had in this life."

Holmes raised an eyebrow. "Indeed?"

"Do you believe in fate, Mr. Holmes?"

"It depends upon what you mean by fate."

"Do you have a brother?"

"Yes, I do."

"And what is he like?"

"Completely unlike me in certain ways, but in others we are very much alike, indeed."

"How so?"

A faint smile flickered across his thin lips.

"We are both of an intellectual turn of mind—in fact, his brain is probably superior to mine."

"He must be quite impressive. And how are you different?"

Holmes's dark eyes searched my face for a moment, then he lowered them and shook his head.

"Except for a certain—aversion to our fellow man, our temperaments could not be more distinct. Whereas I am all nervous energy, kinetic and restless, my brother is a sloth. You may perhaps have remarked upon my rather pronounced leanness."

"That would be difficult not to notice."

"My brother is my exact physical opposite. If you saw the two of us together you would not believe we were related—except perhaps for a certain resemblance around the eyes. I am convinced nothing would please him more than to live the rest of his life seated in his armchair at his club, moving only to turn the pages of a newspaper or order another brandy."

I nodded. "Yes, it is quite astonishing how far apples can fall from the same tree."

Holmes nodded but did not reply. A silence fell between us, heavy with the unasked question.

"And your brother, Mr. Booth?" Holmes said at last, his voice gentle.

"My brother," I began slowly, as if by delaying the words I could somehow delay the thought of those terrible days, "my brother John was very like me some ways—and completely different in others."

"He was a gifted actor, I hear."

"Oh, yes—and handsome, too. All the ladies were in love with him."

"It is hard to imagine one whom Nature has provided with so much being driven to such desperate extremes," Holmes replied. "My apologies if you feel I am prying into matters you would rather not discuss."

I shook my head and lit a cigar. "Thank you for your concern, Mr. Holmes, but my sister Asia insists it does me good to talk about it."

"Perhaps," Holmes murmured. "There are more things in heaven and earth...."

"My brother bore within him a darkness—a hunger, if you will—that was never completely satisfied by what other men would have deemed profuse blessings. Youth, talent, beauty of form and face, a family name of honor and renown—all these gifts were bestowed upon young Johnny, and yet he felt a dissatisfaction with life the rest of us could never understand. He identified always with the South, even though everyone else in our family considered ourselves Northerners. None of us fought in the war, but Johnny seemed determined to rail against the North whenever the chance arose. Then, when victory came to the Union forces, he seemed to come apart in some way. But upon my soul, Mr. Holmes, I will never to this day understand what evil force propelled him to such a desperate and despicable act!"

"Can you not, Mr. Booth?" he replied softly. "You yourself have been considered the pre-eminent actor in this country for most of your career, the sole inheritor of your father's mantle of greatness."

"Perhaps, but Johnny was—"

"Your younger brother, never destined to reach your heights—or so he must have believed."

"But he had fame, and the adoration of women wherever he went."

"But you had the respect and adulation of your peers, the press, and everyone who truly mattered in his eyes. I believe your brother realized he would never be the great tragedian that you are—and having come of age in your shadow, he craved attention more than virtue or honor."

I laughed—a short, bitter exhalation of air. "I swear to you I would exchange all of my renown for a return to the simple pleasures of married life once again. To sit by the fire with my dear Mary once again! That, to me, is real bliss—not dashing madly about from town to town, sleeping in a different bed night after night, eating indifferent food in dull company. To be an actor, Mr. Holmes, is to feel that one's life is never truly one's own."

"Perhaps it is the human condition to be in a state of continual longing—to yearn for what we cannot have."

We talked on into the night. I lost track of time, until I became suddenly aware of the slow, steady clip clop of the milk horse as it plodded down the cobblestone street, and realized that we had stayed up all night. I rose from my chair and pulled the thick drapes aside from the long French windows, and gazed at the faint pink glow in the Eastern sky. I turned to my visitor, sheathed in half-darkness under the gas lights, the lamplight falling on his sharp, aristocratic cheekbones.

I looked out across Gramercy Park, so peaceful and green in the early morning stillness, the air heavy with the scent of mimosa blossoms. The lifting of the cold snap had brought forth a sudden burst of trees blooming all over town. Spring in New York always brought the heavy, sweet aroma of mimosa as the trees surrendered their yellow and white blossoms onto the sidewalks, to be trampled underfoot by scores of passing feet.

I yawned, realizing suddenly how tired I was. My weary body cried out for sweet sleep; I longed to sink into blissful oblivion.

"I hope you don't mind if I leave to retire for the night," I said, "or rather, to sleep away the rest of the morning."

"By all means," Holmes replied. "You must get your rest."

"Good night, then."

"Good night."

I turned and went up the stairs, but could not resist a glance back as I did. My last sight of him was sitting, shrouded in pipe smoke, peering into the half-light of the coming dawn, as if the rising sun itself held the answer to the secrets that plagued us both.

I fell into my bed, feeling a weight had been lifted, but still could not sleep. I tossed and thrashed about for over an hour, and finally, when sleep did come, I drifted in and out of heavy dreams, in which my brother John always seemed to be lurking in the background. Each time I attempted to speak with him, he faded away, shaking his head sadly as his image receded from me.

I awoke to a terrific clap of thunder—shortly afterward, the skies opened up. The rain pelted down with a sharp, percussive sound, like handfuls of pebbles being tossed at the window panes. I watched as the drops hit the glass; defeated in their attack and drained of their energy, they slid harmlessly down the windows. If only my assailant were so easy to overcome—if only I could put up an invisible barrier between us! A deep strain of melancholy threaded through the Booth family like an evil, creeping vine— perhaps it was the price we had to pay for the genius bestowed upon us. As I gazed out at the furious storm, I couldn't help but think of my poor brother—in him the melancholy grew, rampant and untended, into a madness that burst forth in terrible fullness on that fateful night at Ford's Theatre.

Finally I dragged myself out of bed, bathed and dressed myself. Rehearsal had been called for two o'clock in the afternoon, so after a hasty breakfast, Holmes and I took a cab to the theatre.

We were scheduled to rehearse the scene in which Hamlet visits his mother, Gertrude, in her bedroom. He mistakes the busybody Polonius, who is eavesdropping behind a screen, for his Uncle Claudius, who has murdered Hamlet's father. Gertrude calls out for help, and, in a panic, the foolish Polonius echoes her cries. Hamlet hears him and stabs Polonius through the screen, thinking he is stabbing Claudius. In one of the play's many sad ironies, poor Polonius is rewarded for his meddling with an ignominious death, as Hamlet incurs the wrath of the old man's son, Laertes, while the killer Claudius remains free.

In our production, we used a trick sword with a collapsing blade—a simple enough device—so that when I "stabbed" Polonius (Geoff Simmons), the blade retreated into itself, giving the illusion of sinking into his flesh. The effect was very realistic, and audiences invariably gasped when the sword "penetrated" his body.

The scene between Hamlet and his mother was going well—the veteran actress playing Gertrude was wonderful—and when the moment arrived for the stabbing, I was charged with emotion. I spoke Hamlet's lines as he hears Polonius:

How now? a rat?

Dead for a ducat, dead!

I seized the sword from Gertrude's bedside table. It did not feel like the usual prop sword that we used—it was heavier, and the handle felt different. But the moment was fleeting, and I was so hot with emotion that I ignored any misgivings and continued with the scene.

I will never forgive myself for what happened next.

I grasped the sword and plunged it into the curtain Polonius was hiding behind. But instead of the metallic click of the collapsing blade, there was the sickening sound of steel ripping into flesh. Stunned, I pulled my hand back, the sword still clutched in it. It was wet with blood—not stage blood, but real blood. I staggered backward as Geoffrey Simmons stumbled from behind the screen, his face white, clutching his stomach. With a groan, he sank to his knees. He looked up at me with the most pitiful expression of disbelief, hurt and accusation. I tried to speak but could not utter a word. I knelt beside him and caught him in my arms; I was vaguely aware of a woman screaming behind me. And then all was blackness; it was as though someone had pulled a shade over my eyes, and I lost consciousness.

The next thing I knew I was on the divan in my dressing room, Holmes bending over me. Squinting in an attempt to focus my eyes, I tried to sit up.

"Easy, now," Holmes said. "Don't try to stand just yet. You've had a shock—we all have."

"Geoffrey!" I cried. "Is he—?"

"I'm afraid he did not survive the wound," Holmes replied gently. "Everyone believes it was an accident."

"It was no accident," I said grimly.

"Yes, I know. Someone put that sword there on purpose."

"But why kill poor Geoffrey?"

"Clearly he knows something. That is no doubt why he left the note asking to speak with you." He began pacing the room, his face dark. "We must act decisively, and soon."

It struck me at that we were caught in the same dilemma as Shakespeare's famous character: to act or not to act—and when?

When I recovered from my shock, I made a brief appearance in front of the rest of the company to announce that rehearsal was canceled indefinitely—at least until we found a new Polonius. I was careful to call the event a "horrible accident," and cautioned everyone to check his or her props carefully from now on. Perhaps others had suspicions this was no accident, but if so, they did not tell me.

Holmes and I hailed a cab—I sat in moody silence as it rattled through the streets. I now was in a moral quandary, and had to seriously consider canceling the entire production. I had thought up until now that I was the only one in danger, but clearly I was mistaken.

No sooner had we seated ourselves in the grill room when Hector handed me my mail. In it was a bill from the theatre owner for our monthly rent, which made my decision even more painful. If I did not present Hamlet, the bill would go unpaid and my entire company would be out of work. I sighed deeply and tossed the letter on the table next to me.

"What is it?" Holmes asked.

"A bill from our landlord. Each year he threatens to sell the building, and each year I find a way to dissuade him. He claims if he turned it into a store, it would be much more profitable."

"No doubt he is right," Holmes answered. "I wonder why he continues to operate it as a theatre."

"I suspect prestige has something to do with it."

"Of course," Holmes agreed. "He can boast at parties that he is Edwin Booth's landlord…which makes me wonder."

"Wonder what?"

"I had previously discarded money as a motive, but perhaps I should revise my thinking. There may be an unseen player in this affair, after all."

I was about to respond, but at that moment the door opened and in strode Lawrence Barrett.

Barrett and I had known each other for many years, since my earliest days in New York. He was an intense and gifted actor, but a difficult and demanding man. We had had many ups and downs over the years—after one quarrel we didn't speak for half a year. I had refused to cast him in a lead I felt he was unsuited for, and it was months before he forgave me. He was as covetous of fame as I was weary of it. His Cassius in Julius Caesar was renowned—he was suited to the part as few actors are, being himself not only lean but a truly ambitious and "hungry" nature. Though a critically acclaimed actor, he never drew large audiences as I did, which rankled him terribly.

He swung into the room on his long legs, wearing a forest green wool cape and shiny black riding boots. He looked around the room haughtily, no doubt hoping to be recognized by some young actor who might ask him for an autograph. No one paid him any attention, though, and he flicked his cape over his shoulder, much as a cat flicks its tail when irritated. Spying me, he stalked stiff-legged to our table; a frown passed across his face when he saw Holmes.

"Hello, Larry," I said.

"Good day, Edwin," he replied, still staring at Holmes.

"Allow me to present Mr. Sherlock Holmes. He is our Horatio for this production. Holmes, this is Lawrence—"

"Lawrence Barrett," Holmes interrupted smoothly. "I had the pleasure of seeing your Cassius once—I found it to be the definitive interpretation of the role."

"You flatter me, sir," Barrett replied, coloring. He had a broad Irish face, with a Cupid's bow mouth, rosy cheeks and a fair complexion that betrayed his emotions. (It was rumored his father's name was Brannigan, but that he changed it for his stage career.)

"I think not," Holmes answered, "though your modesty becomes you."

I held my tongue—Barrett was a gifted man, but modesty was not in his repertoire.

"In any case," Holmes continued, "It is an honor to meet you."

"Thank you, sir," Barrett replied, somewhat placated, but I sensed his uneasiness.

"Won't you join us?" I said.

"No, thank you—I have urgent business; however, I heard of your terrible accident, and I wished to offer you my services as Polonius."

(Barrett was five years younger than myself—as my critics liked to point out, I was long in the tooth for the role of Hamlet, though I continued to draw crowds in that role more than any other.)

"What a capital idea," I replied.

"I have just ended an out-of-town engagement, as it happens, and am quite free at the moment," Barrett said, all the while flicking his cape nervously. It occurred to me that possibly there was no "out of town engagement," and that Larry was in need of a job. I knew the man too well to puncture his pride needlessly, however, so I nodded seriously.

"How kind of you to think of me. Can you start immediately?"

"Indeed I can," he replied.

"Tomorrow at noon, then?"

"That will be fine. And now if you'll excuse me, I have some business to attend to. It was a pleasure meeting you," he said, addressing Holmes.

"The pleasure was all mine," Holmes replied.

"Until tomorrow, then," Barrett said, bowing slightly.

"Yes—thank you, Larry," I answered.

His mouth curled upwards in a smile, and again I was reminded of a cat—precise, wary, watchful. "Always a pleasure to help out a friend."

"He does indeed have a lean and hungry look," Holmes remarked when Barrett had gone.

"Yes," I answered. "He was born to play Cassius."

"How long was he in the military?"

By now, I had become so used to Holmes's pronouncements that I displayed no reaction.

"About four years, I believe, during the war," I responded casually.

"An officer—a captain, perhaps, or major," Holmes said.

"Captain."

He looked at me as if expecting the usual questions and pronouncements of astonishment, but I refused to play along.

"Now then," I said, enjoying the faint expression of disappointment that crossed his face, "what are you going to order for dinner?"

But we were both exhausted emotionally and physically, and neither of us ate much. By the time we were ready to retire I was yawning uncontrollably. I settled into my comfortable four-poster bed and closed my eyes, but before I drifted off to sleep, two unwelcome thoughts occurred to me: that as a cavalry officer, Barrett was presumably a very good shot, and furthermore, perhaps not all was as forgiven as I had hoped.

My mood was not improved when I arrived at my dressing room the next day to find a piece of paper nailed to the door. Trembling, I plucked it off and read it, instantly recognizing Richard's Act III speech from "Richard II":

> For God's sake, let us sit upon the ground
> And tell sad stories of the death of kings;
> How some have been deposed; some slain in war,
> Some haunted by the ghosts they have deposed;
> Some poisoned by their wives: some sleeping killed;
> All murdered.

I turned to see Holmes coming toward me, and handed him the note without speaking. He glanced at it, then shook his head.

"Someone is toying with you."

"Maybe it is time to admit defeat and cancel the production," I said reluctantly. I could no longer think clearly; I was physically and spiritually exhausted.

"If you can grant me one more day," Holmes said, "I think I can flush out your assailant. However, should you decide to give up, I certainly understand—"

"Very well," I interrupted him. "At the end of today, though, I must make the decision."

The bell rang for rehearsal, and we headed off down the corridor toward the stage. Today we were to rehearse the final duel scene; I for one was not sure I was up to the task.

All good actors must immerse themselves in the emotional life of their character, while keeping a part of their brain detached, so they may remember their lines, as well as execute any blocking and stage business. This "double life" extends to their attitude toward their fellow actors: Othello, for example, must experience all the torment of jealous passion toward poor Desdemona, at the same time taking care not to actually strangle her during their final scene. Of course, these lines have been crossed—I myself have more than once had to restrain my impulse to actually choke another actor onstage, and have come away with bruises more than once from a fight scene that got out of hand.

Nowhere is a combination of control and restraint more necessary than in the final scene of Hamlet. During the duel between Laertes and Hamlet in front of the entire Danish court, each must give and receive a nick of the sword which must appear to pierce the skin. Unbeknownst to Hamlet, Laertes's sword has been dipped in a deadly poison, so when Hamlet receives what he imagines to be nothing more than a tiny scratch, he has in fact been poisoned. Later, when Hamlet seizes Laertes's sword—still unaware it is coated with poison—he inflicts a minor cut upon his friend, not knowing he has fatally wounded him.

It has always been my desire to create as much realism as possible, so I provide myself and Laertes with a small pouch of stage blood to be held in the left hand during the sword play—then, at the proper time, the pouch is clapped on the area of the "wound," creating a very realistic effect for the audience. I have heard gasps from the gallery during these moments—a sound that is music to the ears of any actor/manager.

Nate Carlisle was a superior swordsman, and though my duel with him had been carefully staged, I was always on my guard. As we squared off for the duel, I thought I saw a gleam in his eyes I had not noticed before—or perhaps it was a trick of the light, the glare of the hot gas lamps catching his eye just so.

We crossed swords and began our duel. The actors playing members of the Danish court were on stage with us, including Gertrude and Claudius. I could see the rest of the company watching from the wings—including Lawrence Barrett, who was observing with a keen expression on his face. He had come to the theatre, even though his scenes were not scheduled for rehearsal.

It was not unusual for other actors to watch the duel scene, but for some reason I felt a shiver trickle down my spine as I touched swords with Nate.

At first, the scene ran exactly as we had rehearsed it—but when the moment came for the first "touch," when Laertes nicks Hamlet with what turns out to be a fatal wound, to my surprise, Nate seemed to lose his balance, and his sword actually raked across my face.

My left cheek stinging, I brought my hand to my face. There was a murmur from the wings, and I thought I heard several of the women gasp.

"Sorry!" Nate panted. "I lost my balance. Are you all right?"

"I'm fine," I replied.

"Shall we stop?"

"No, no," I said. "Let's continue."

I glanced at Holmes, who, as Horatio, was standing to one side of the other Danish courtiers. I thought I saw him nod almost imperceptibly, but perhaps I was mistaken. I returned to the duel.

It seemed to me that Nate was fighting with more vigor than usual—he huffed and sweated and leapt from side to side; more than once I had to dodge an unusually vigorous swipe of his sword. I almost stopped to ask what had gotten into him, but something inside me prevented it—a desire to not lose face in front of the rest of the company, maybe; or perhaps it was a darker, more self-destructive impulse. When the moment came for Hamlet and Laertes to exchange swords—thus giving Hamlet the poisoned sword, he suddenly changed the blocking and leapt toward me. Reacting completely on instinct, I dodged out of the way, dropped to the floor and rolled to the other side of the stage, only to come up to see him charging at me.

"Nate!" I panted. "For god's sake, what are you doing?"

But he roared with rage and kept coming at me. I rolled in the other direction—I had dropped my sword and was defenseless. Backed up against the wall, I was cornered. I saw the glint of his steel blade headed toward my face, and closed my eyes, expecting the blow.

But it did not come.

When I opened my eyes, I saw Holmes had taken up my sword and was fighting with Nate.

"Holmes!" I cried.

"Stay clear!" he yelled back.

I had no choice but to obey. The blades were flashing silver in the stage lights, and to come anywhere near them was to risk serious injury. Though Holmes was clearly a skilled swordsman, Nate's rage had turned him into a madman, and he sliced and jabbed with the fury of a man fighting to the death. It was all Holmes could do to stave off his vicious attack, parrying each thrust with an alert desperation. The rest of the company hovered in the wings, cowed by Nate's rage. I grabbed a theatre page by the arm.

"Run and fetch the police!" I exclaimed.

The boy nodded at me, his eyes wide with terror.

"Now!" I bellowed. "RUN!"

He scampered down the stairs and out through the theatre toward the front entrance. I turned back to the stage, where to my horror I watched Nate back Holmes into the opposite corner of the stage.

"Now," he panted, lifting his sword over his head, "you will die, too!"

Hardly aware of what I was doing, I sprang to my feet and hurled my body through the air, landing on Nate with a thud, knocking him to the ground. He writhed and fought like a rabid beast, clawing and kicking at me. But Holmes snatched his sword, and three or four other members of the cast—including Larry

Barrett—threw themselves upon him, helping me to subdue him. We wrestled him to his feet—he continued to struggle, but he was outnumbered now, and we managed to hold him.

"Are you all right, Edwin?" Barrett asked, true concern in his voice.

"Yes, Larry—quite all right, thank you."

Nate Carlisle strained against his captors, trying vainly to wrest himself free. "Damn you, Edwin Booth—why aren't you dead?" he panted. To my surprise, his accent had changed—it was now decidedly Southern.

"I took the liberty of removing your sword from backstage and replacing it with another one," Holmes said to him.

Nate turned his gaze on Holmes. "Damn you!" he gasped, still quite out of breath.

I stared at Holmes, confused.

"He had poisoned it," Holmes told me. "So when he cut your face, he expected you to die—and when you didn't, his plan was thrown off."

I heard a collective gasp from the rest of the company.

"So it was no accident?" I said.

"Oh, no," Holmes said. "Though he hoped it would look like one—just another unfortunate accident."

Nate glared at Holmes and struggled, but his fellow actors held him firmly. "You—you—what are you, a wizard?"

"I am merely one who observes," Holmes responded.

"I don't understand, Nate," I said. "Why would you want to kill me?"

"My dear Booth," Holmes began, laying a hand on my shoulder.

"No—I want to hear," I said, pulling away from him and facing Nate. "What I have I ever done to you?"

He wrenched a hand free and pulled a locket from his neck, throwing it at my feet. "This is my sister Daisy—the poor unfortunate girl your brother ruined. The day she died, I vowed a Booth would die to avenge her!"

"But what have I to do with any of this?"

"Your wretched brother discarded her like he did so many other women," he replied in a voice choked with rage. "She never recovered, and when he shot Lincoln, she went mad from grief."

"How is this my f-fault?" I stammered, my childhood affliction once again returning.

"Do you have any notion what it is like to endure the humiliation of Reconstruction? 'Reconstruction'—ha! What a bitter joke!" He spat out the words, his eyes blazing with fury. "Lincoln was a tyrant, but when your brother killed him, the North took revenge upon us by humiliating us. If your cursed brother had not murdered that mountebank, things might have gone differently. My poor mother died of grief and hardship! She never recovered from my sister's madness—I watched her steady decline, until at last she died of a broken heart."

"But I could not have prevented my brother's—"

"If you had not been so absorbed in your own career, your fame, you might have noticed what he was planning! You were as blind to your own kin as a cart horse!"

"B-but I—" Once again I began to stutter painfully.

Holmes stepped forward once again and laid a hand on my arm.

"There is nothing more to be learned from this man," he said in a low voice. "His mind is addled."

I knew he was right, yet I could not take my eyes from his face, red and twisted with fury. I felt I was somehow looking at my brother Johnny's face. I was aware of Holmes's hand on my arm, gently pulling me away, as half a dozen uniformed policemen strode purposefully down the aisles of the theatre. The assembled company stood watching them in silence as they climbed the stairs to the stage. It was as if we were the stunned spectators of a tragic play, waiting passively to see what would happen next.

"This is your man, Sergeant," Holmes said to the burly, red-headed Sergeant.

The sergeant nodded and turned to his men, who quickly and expertly cuffed Carlisle's hands behind his back and began to lead him away. He wrenched himself free for a moment and pivoted unsteadily back toward us.

"A curse on you and your family, Edwin Booth!" he managed to cry before the policemen dragged him away.

The red-haired sergeant approached me and coughed delicately.

"When you have a moment, we'd like to take a statement from you, Mr. Booth," he said respectfully.

"Of course," I replied, feeling light-leaded with the unreal sensation I was awaking from a horrible dream.

The sergeant turned to leave, then, appearing to think better of it, turned back again.

"Uh, I—that is, well, sir, I want to say how much I enjoyed your Brutus in Julius Caesar last week. My wife, she…well, I wonder, sir, if you would mind—perhaps this isn't the time, but…." He fumbled in his pocket and extracted a small black notebook. On the cover "NYPD" was embossed in gold lettering. "If you could just—it's for my wife, you understand, sir."

The sergeant's face was a deep crimson, and he was sweating at the collar of his tight wool uniform.

"Of course, Sergeant," I said, touched by his discomfort. I myself was often ill at ease in social situations, and though both of my Marys had been taken from me—the first by death, the second by madness—how well I knew the bliss of having a wife to come home to.

I signed the paper and pressed it into the Sergeant's perspiring palms.

"Love her well," I said. "Love her and care for her with all your heart."

He looked at me, transparent pearls of sweat gathering on his broad forehead.

"I will—th-thank you, sir," he stammered, running a hand through his bristle of red hair. He grasped my hand and shook it vigorously. "Best of luck, sir."

With that, he turned and stumbled off after his officers. The company members stood in silence for a few moments, then a low murmur began among them. They all seemed to be in shock, understandably, and I called off rehearsal for the rest of the day. They were quiet at first, still stunned by the sudden violence, but by the time everyone had their coats on, they were bursting with questions and demands for explanations. Some of them were making plans to head off for Tom's Tavern, a favorite watering-hole for theatre folks, run by a former actor named, improbably enough, Thomas Lawless. Several of them importuned Holmes and myself to join them. As is true of all actors, they thrived on drama no less than the sound of their own voices, and now that the danger had passed, they could savor the aftermath of all the excitement in endless discussions, digressions, and dissections—and, best of all, countless drafts of whatever Tom happened to have in stock.

However, I wanted nothing more than to sit and stare into the fireplace at the Players, a glass of brandy in my hand, the ever faithful Hector at my side.

Holmes and I hailed a cab and made our way back to the club. I said very little during the ride, being preoccupied with my own thoughts. Perhaps sensing my need for silence, Holmes stared out the window into the darkening streets.

When we were settled in front of the fire, I spoke at last.

"I want to thank you for everything you have done, Holmes—I think it's fair to say that you saved not only my life, but also—"

He silenced me with a wave of his hand. "I do not feel I was successful at all; after all, a man died because of my inability to anticipate the deviousness of this killer."

"Poor Geoffrey," I said. "He must have known something, and that's why he was killed."

"Yes," Holmes agreed. "But what did he know?"

"Does it matter now?"

He frowned and drummed his fingers on the arm of his chair. "I am not yet satisfied that this affair is entirely over. There are one or two points I find most disturbing."

"How did you know Nate had poisoned his sword?"

"After the first disaster with poor Geoffrey, I kept a very close eye on all the props—especially the swords. And I took the liberty of following Nate Carlisle after rehearsal yesterday, where he happened to pay a visit to a pharmacy."

"So you think he bought the poison then?"

"I went in afterward myself on the pretext of needing some valerian root, and managed to have a look at the receipt when the chemist's back was turned. It was a curare derivative—very rare and very deadly. A paralytic agent which, shortly after entering the bloodstream, causes paralysis and death. There is no known antidote. This was an example of life imitating art—a very deadly example."

A thin, cold shiver slithered down my spine as I realized the truth of his statement, and I suddenly felt the full impact of my narrow escape.

"I am astounded that Nate knew his poisons so thoroughly," I said.

Holmes shook his head. "I am not so certain he did. The use of this obscure and powerful poison suggests the hand of another agent."

"But what—"

"Not what, my dear Booth—who. I sense someone else's hand behind all this—someone far more deadly than young Nate Carlisle."

"Why do you say that?"

He paused to draw on his pipe before answering. The smoke from the pipe curled upward, a thin grey mist partially obscuring his face.

"I am not convinced that Nate Carlisle was capable of so much patience and planning…from what I saw of him, he does not seem up to it. I have the feeling he was a pawn of some larger, more cold-blooded agent…and yet I cannot quite…" His voice trailed off, and he stared in the direction of the French windows at the front of the building.

"What makes you say that?"

"Did you remark upon how upset he was when poor Kitty's dog died from the poison he had intended for you?"

"Yes, but perhaps he was just acting."

"But why call attention to himself? If he truly felt no remorse, wouldn't he simply say nothing?"

"I take your point. If his guilt was genuine, what does that suggest to you?"

"Merely that he is no natural killer. What he did, he did with some reluctance, accounting perhaps in part for his high rate of failure."

"How did you know he would use the poison on the sword?"

"I didn't know for certain—that's why I had to find out what would happen if I switched the swords. It wasn't enough that he bought the poison—that in itself is no crime, and he could always claim that he purchased it to poison rats or some other vermin. No, he had to be caught red-handed, as it were."

"What made you suspect him in the first place?"

"In some ways it was a process of elimination. But one or two things he said or did led me to think he was the most likely culprit."

"Such as—?"

"I already mentioned his pronounced grief at the death of Kitty's dog, and his attempt to console her, which struck me as unusual, unless he was somehow responsible."

"What else?"

"His background was shadowy. He came to you on recommendation from a theatre company in Savannah."

"Yes. He presented me with a letter."

"How well do you know that city?"

"Not well. I traveled there once with my father."

"I sent a telegram to the address on that letter, and there is no such theatre."

"Good heavens—my poor Mary always said I was too trusting of people."

"You are a very busy man. Savannah is far enough away that you would be unlikely to check on that reference—and he must have known that."

"True; I often hire actors on a single recommendation. I can always fire them if they are inadequate."

"That is precisely what young Carlisle was counting on—which is why he came with his part perfectly learned. As you pointed out, he is quite a good actor, so you were not likely to fire him. And, I suspect, faking a recommendation is perhaps not unusual in the theatrical community."

I sighed ruefully. "You're right—even had I found out the letter was false, I still probably would have chalked it up to the eagerness of a young actor to find employment."

Holmes smiled. "There was one more thing."

"What was that?"

"As I just remarked, he is a gifted actor."

"Yes, that's true. But what—?"

"And he did a credible job of pretending to be a Northerner."

"Yes, his accent was quite convincing."

"I agree—except for one small thing."

"What's that?"

"He made one small slip. When the cast was ordering breakfast the other day, he asked for 'a egg.' Not 'an egg,' but 'a egg.'"

"How odd. But I don't see what that—"

"In certain parts of the South, that is a very common usage. However, it is virtually unknown in the North, which made me suspect he was not all he claimed to be."

I shook my head. "But that's such a small detail."

"My dear Booth, details may be small, but they are anything but insignificant. They can indeed be the difference between life and death." He drew in more smoke from his pipe, a thoughtful expression on his lean face. "You own your theatre building, do you not?"

"Yes, I do."

"And have there been any attempts to purchase it from you recently?"

"Well, now that you mention it—I had an offer a few months ago which I turned down."

"Have you had any suspicious fires since then, by any chance?"

I stared at him. "How did you know? We had a fire in the middle of the night, just over two months ago—luckily a stage hand had fallen asleep in the wings and gave the alarm; the fire station is only half a block away. We only lost a few costumes and some scenery."

He nodded slowly. "Yes...I think I am beginning to see."

"See what?"

"A motive. It is not yourself that this criminal is after at all—it is your building. You were merely in the way."

"But why on earth would someone go to such extremes to get that particular building?"

"Precisely, my dear Booth. Why, indeed?"

Just then Hector entered the room with a letter on a silver tray. I began to reach for it, but he handed it to Holmes.

"Thank you, Hector," Holmes said, taking the letter. "Who gave this to you?"

"It was a tall man, sir—as tall as yourself. Skinny as a rail, too, with a neck like a chicken, and a big ol' head atop it. Didn't look to me as though a head like that belonged on such a skinny little neck—it seemed 'bout like to topple right off, I thought."

"Thank you. Anything else?"

"His eyes, sir—they was deep and hooded, like...like a big ol' rattler, sir. That's what he brought to mind, sir—a big ol' rattler sunnin' hisself on a rock, with his head swivelin' from side to side as though he was lookin' for some poor field mouse to devour."

Holmes smiled. "Thank you, Hector—you are a remarkably observant man."

Holmes's praise seemed to put wind in Hector's elocutionary sails, and, encouraged, he waxed on. "I didn't like him, sir—no, sir, I didn't like him one little bit. Felt like if I turned my back on him, the big ol' snake would gulp me down in one bite. I'd watch out for him if I were you, sir."

"Thank you, Hector—I shall heed your warning," Holmes replied earnestly.

Hector left the room muttering to himself about rattlesnakes disguised as men. Holmes watched him depart, then turned to me.

"He is quite a remarkable man, your servant," he said.

"Yes, I know."

Holmes turned his attention to the note in his hand. He read it quickly and handed it to me. It was written on the finest quality stationary, a creamy white parchment—the letterhead was embossed with gold initials: JFM.

A note was etched in a firm masculine hand in blue ink.

> My congratulations—you win this round. I assume you have deduced by now that young Carlisle was merely a pawn; perhaps you have even surmised my motive in enlisting his aid. It is quite simple: I needed the building for my own purposes. If you want to know more, I will be happy to meet with you a week from now in Chicago. (Of course, I cannot guarantee your safety should you take me up on my offer.) I have decided to move on to—shall we say—less crowded pastures. The river is no longer worth crossing with Chiron standing guard over the prize.
>
> In any case, I am certain we shall meet again, and I look forward to crossing swords sometime in the future.
>
> Yours,
> James F. Moriarty

I gazed up at Holmes, who was looking very pensive.

"Chiron," he murmured.

"Isn't he the centaur who gave up his immortality in order to save Prometheus?"

"I see you know your Greek mythology."

"What a curious reference. Who is this person?"

"He is obviously educated, brilliant and ruthless. I have a feeling this is not the last the world will hear of him."

"So is this the missing piece of the puzzle?"

"I believe it is," Holmes replied. "He has supplied the missing piece—and I suspect he also created the entire puzzle."

That the world would know of him is a matter of record—and of course, before long, the world would also know of Sherlock Holmes. He left New York soon after our production closed, and some months later I received a postcard from him, sent from Chicago, complaining it was too windy and that he much preferred New York. After that I heard nothing—until I began following his exploits in London some years later.

As for me, I went back to my life as an actor without further incident. My part in the ongoing life and adventures of the great detective was over…the rest is silence.

FOOL'S GOLD

by Martin Rosenstock

In my endeavour to render truthfully the methods by which my friend, Sherlock Holmes, arrived at solutions to some of the most intricate cases, I have focused on the scientific side of his character. Undoubtedly, it is the remarkable amount of knowledge that he commands in such areas of human inquiry as chemistry, botany, and anatomy that accounts for much of the success he has achieved. However, I desire not to lay myself open to the charge that I present a skewed portrait of his character; therefore, I should like to emphasize that Holmes is also a shrewd reader of the human soul. These few sentences may suffice as a preface, and I now turn to the task of reconstructing from my notes a case which was solved not only by my friend's understanding of the laws by which the natural world operates, but also by his ability to discern that ephemeral world concealed in each and every one of us.

"Ah, good morning, Watson," said Holmes, as I walked into the living room of our quarters in 221B Baker Street. "You had better hurry up with your breakfast. Lestrade sent word. He will be stopping by shortly."

Mrs Hudson was already pouring my tea. I sat down and lifted a warm scone from the basket in the centre of the table.

"I trust you have an idea as to the nature of the inspector's call."

My companion exhaled smoke from a cigar, adding to the cloud that was already hovering below the ceiling. "Well, it would appear our dear Lestrade has once again followed a trail till it turned cold."

I sipped my tea and looked out of the window. It was a fine spring morning. Small white clouds were moving at a brisk pace eastward across a pale blue sky. It rained heavily during the night, and the downpour cleared the London air. The yellow brickwork of the house across the street shone brightly. In the distance a dog was barking.

"Don't you remember the murder that caused such consternation on Monday?" Holmes continued.

He was in high spirits, I noticed now that Mrs Hudson's tea had chased away the last vestiges of sleep. His grey eyes shone with the gleam of anticipation I had so often observed before.

At that moment, the doorbell rang, and Mrs Hudson could be heard going to answer it.

Recalling an article I had read in *The Times*, I asked: "Neville Cavendish?"

Steps were coming up the staircase.

"Precisely, my dear Watson," said Holmes, then lifted an index finger to his lips in a gesture that betokened silence on the content of our conversation.

There was a sharp knock on the door, and Lestrade stepped into the room. "Mr Holmes, good morning." He nodded to me. "Dr Watson, good morning to you, too. I am sorry to be interrupting your breakfast."

"Not at all," I said. "Urgency is a feature of your profession, Inspector. Please don't mind me. I shall enjoy the privilege of listening quietly while you and Holmes discuss the business at hand. Would you care for a cup of tea?"

"Too kind of you. But no thank you, Dr Watson."

Mrs Hudson had taken Lestrade's hat and coat, and Holmes was now ushering him to an easy chair opposite his own. The inspector sat down, but did not lean back to make himself comfortable. Rather, he remained bent forward with his lower arms resting on his thighs. His fingers were clenched. The usually dapper and wiry man, I now realized, looked positively exhausted. Dark shadows lay below his eyes, and his frame seemed to be sagging.

"I am sure you know why I've come by to bother you this morning," he began, somewhat sheepishly.

I expected that Holmes would grasp at this opportunity to demonstrate that Lestrade could dispense with the explanations, since the cause of his visit was as well known to us as his failure was apparent. However, my companion seemed to be in a forgiving mood, and to my astonishment waived airily:

"I am sure I have no idea whatsoever, Lestrade. I've spent the last few days measuring my skills as a violinist against Brahms's *Concerto in D*, and once music seizes hold of me I tend to forget the world at large."

"Ah, I see," said the inspector, an expression of relief crossing his face. "Well, then let me fill you in on this sordid affair."

Much of the information had already been in the paper. Some details, however, the police had kept secret, as public knowledge of the investigation's minutiae could only help the criminal.

Neville Cavendish was found dead by his butler on Monday morning. The Major General's body lay in his study, a few yards from a safe that had been forced open. He had been hit in the face with a blunt instrument, probably a tool of some sort. The blow had shattered his left cheekbone, but had not been lethal. Subsequently, however, the intruder had shot Cavendish through the head, using a cushion from a nearby sofa to stifle the report. It had been murder, cold-blooded and merciless.

"The revolver lay beside the body," Lestrade continued. "It was Cavendish's own service revolver. It appears the Major General got home around ten on Sunday evening. He had not been expected till Wednesday. He'd been off fly-fishing in Wales. But the trout weren't rising, this according to the clerk at the hotel in which he was staying. Cavendish wasn't the most patient man, and so early on Sunday morning he packed his bags and boarded the train from Swansea to Bristol and then took the express to Paddington. That evening, when he opened his front door, he most likely heard the burglar working on the safe. He fetched his revolver, which he kept in a cupboard by his bedside, and went to confront the intruder. Whoever it was, he seems to have nerves of steel. Cavendish must have had the gun pointed at him, but he brought the old man to the floor..."

"...and put a bullet through his head," Holmes concluded.

"Exactly."

"Why did Cavendish not send a wire that he would be returning early?"

"Ah," said Lestrade, "of course, I asked the same question. It appears he in fact did send a wire. However, Cavendish only kept a small household, with one butler. A lady comes in twice a week to clean and do the laundry. The butler is one Jacob Fitzsimmons, a man in his middle years, and I am afraid that the mouse was playing while the cat was away. Fitzsimmons appears to be romantically involved with a young seamstress, and he and the girl took the opportunity afforded by Mr Cavendish's absence to go to Salisbury for the weekend. On Sunday night, they were guests at an inn, under a false name. Be that as it may, it accounts for the fact that no one was at home when the telegraph boy came by to deliver the Major General's wire."

Holmes exhaled smoke. "I see, Lestrade. Pray continue."

"Well, Fitzsimmons returned to Cavendish's house around eleven on Monday morning and discovered the body. The Major General's physician, Dr Lanyon, lives across the street. Fitzsimmons ran to fetch him. The doctor came right away, but Cavendish was beyond help. Lanyon appears to have been quite upset; he and the Major General were good friends. Then the butler went to alert the police." Lestrade pressed thumb and forefinger against his tired eyes. "Cavendish's murderer got what he wanted. Whether he opened the safe before or after the murder we do not know. But the only contents left were a number of stock certificates impossible to sell anonymously, the Major General's stamp collection, and..." Lestrade cleared his throat, "...a few pictures of a somewhat lurid nature, all rather old."

Holmes turned to me. "What say you, Watson?"

I had been listening so intently to the inspector's account that I had forgotten my scone. It was cold to the touch, as I now took a few seconds to sift through my thoughts.

"Well," I ventured, "do we know what the murderer stole?"

"We have a good idea of it," replied Lestrade. "At least if Cavendish's sister is to be believed. It appears he never showed her the safe's contents, but mentioned that he had put his late wife's jewellery there, which in itself was worth a fortune; you might recall the society columns frequently praised Mrs Cavendish's exquisite appearance. The jewellery is insured, but beyond that Miss Cavendish claims that her brother also alluded to keeping a substantial amount of gold bullion there."

"Gold bullion?!" I exclaimed. "At home?"

"That's what she says."

"Miss Cavendish is *the* Miss Cavendish?" Holmes inquired.

"Afraid so," the inspector nodded.

I whistled through my teeth.

"I think it is time we had a look at the scene of the crime," said my companion.

"Very good." The inspector rose from his chair. "That will also give you a chance to meet the lady in question. She will be at the house, as will the butler, Fitzsimmons."

We were all silent for a good ten minutes, as our cab rattled towards Mayfair. Half London seemed to be up and about. Ladies in fine dress were inspecting the wares laid out in shop windows, gentlemen were strolling the sidewalks, cigar in hand; I noticed postmen delivering letters, workers behind a truck shovelling coal into a cellar, a flower girl accosting a young toff, newspaper boys crying out headlines, a shabbily dressed character eyeing a matron's handbag, and on every corner vendors were hawking their produce. Between the milling crowds, there scampered street urchins, always on the lookout for a dropped penny or an apple that might be swiped from a pushcart. So much life, so much activity, in such a narrowly circumscribed arena! London seemed like a vast machine at full steam, though not running entirely without friction. But then again, perhaps it was the very fact that some of the machine's myriad components were not fitted perfectly that kept the whole monstrous thing chugging along.

Holmes spoke up: "You knew Cavendish, didn't you, Watson?"

"I would not go so far as to say I knew him. Perhaps we shook hands twice in a club in Bombay. He also went to Afghanistan, though our paths never crossed there."

"How did he strike you?" asked Lestrade.

I do not care to dwell much on the years of my life spent in the East, seeing as how they contain few pleasant memories. Now, however, I made an effort to resurrect the images of the past. There had been a reception of some form or another, all gentlemen in gala uniform, their wives in evening dress, much toasting with champagne. I had had a touch of fever and was awaiting the time when I could retire. Neville Cavendish and his wife sat across from me at a large round table. She, a short, rather plain looking woman with sandy hair and a pale complexion, was making conversation with a gentleman next to her. Cavendish, heavy set with fleshy jowls and a reddish-brown moustache, was quietly eating his steak, while listening to the conversation unfolding to his side, or at least pretending to do so.

"He was rather unassuming, if I recall correctly," I now said, "for a military man. When I later read of his bravery in the field, at Sherpur and Maiwand, I was somewhat surprised. Of course, I should have known better. When I met him—it must have been in '78 or '79—he was already quite famous."

Lestrade nodded. "The Empire was built by men like him. I've looked into his biography. He was everywhere. Malaya, Guiana, Sierra Leone, the Far East, India…" The inspector trailed off.

"A man who might have made many enemies throughout his life," I suggested.

"That may be so," Lestrade agreed. "But what is certain is that he also made many friends, and has many admirers. The press has been hounding me the entire week. Also, I've received communication by well-placed people indicating that they expect this case to be cleared up as fast as possible."

"What have you done to that effect?" asked Holmes.

"The obvious. I'm having all the fences in London shadowed, everyone who might be capable of moving such a haul. Also, I'm requiring lists of new sellers from every jeweller and gold dealer. But my hope rests on the diamonds. Lloyds holds detailed descriptions, and in their present form the stones can hardly be sold. They will have to be re-cut, and there are only a few men who might be willing to undertake such a task if the provenance of the stones cannot be established. Most of these men reside in Antwerp. The ports from which ships leave to Belgium are being watched, and I have contacted my Belgian colleagues to request their assistance. So far nothing has come of it," he added, dejection in his voice.

While Lestrade spoke, the cab drew up before a red-brick Georgian mansion. We alighted, and the inspector paid the fare. A constable in uniform was standing guard outside a wrought-iron gate, presumably to keep the purveyors of news at bay. Lestrade gave him a curt nod and we stepped onto the premises.

"The criminal entered through the back of the house," the inspector said, as we walked up the gravel path towards the main entrance. "He broke open the kitchen door. It only has a cheap lock that offered no resistance."

As we neared the portico, Lestrade nodded to the right, "Follow me." He led the way along the side of the house. Boxwood and rose bushes had been planted two yards from the wall and only left a narrow passage. The scent of blossoms filled the air, and birds flitted amongst the branches. It was hard to imagine that only a few days ago this house, situated in an idyllic setting that allowed one to forget the hubbub of London, had been the scene of a grisly murder.

We turned a corner, and the inspector pointed.

"It's been a few days, of course, but I made sure to leave things as we found them."

"Well, let's have a look," sighed Holmes and stepped forward to inspect the door. Its white paint was peeling in some areas; two squares of glass, both intact, formed the upper quarter. The lock had been rudely forced, probably with a crowbar jammed between the door and the frame. The face-plate was hanging from one screw. The other one had broken as the latch bolt gave way under the pressure.

My companion examined the nut and spindle in a cursory fashion, then focused his eyes on an area of the door a foot and half above the lock. About where an average man's shoulder might be, the paint had been scuffed, exposing the underlying wood, and the dent made by a crowbar was clearly visible.

"I've seen enough," said Holmes. "Please lead the way to the study, Lestrade."

We stepped into a scrupulously clean kitchen and from there into a hallway that led to the vestibule. To our left the grand staircase rose to the first floor. A deep carpet showing Indian motifs in red and golden hues covered the steps. On the walls hung items that testified to a lifetime spent in the colonies. Hunting trophies, African masks, rifles, spears, knives and swords, two Massai shields, the head-dress of a South-American Indian, a blow tube, framed maps, and paintings of various land and sea engagements covered every square foot of space. There seemed to be a loose geographical order to the collection.

As we climbed the stairs, a door opened somewhere above us, and a man dressed in a butler's uniform appeared at the top of the landing. "Good day, gentleman," he said in a rich baritone, as we reached the final steps.

"Jacob Fitzsimmons," the inspector introduced. "You will recall, he discovered the body."

The butler, a stoutly built, handsome man, bowed slightly. Some streaks of grey on his temples belied his youthful, ruddy complexion. I guessed him to be in his late thirties. "It is a distinct honour to meet you, sirs," he said.

Holmes and I politely nodded to our new acquaintance. I had caught a trace of an Irish brogue and thus added: "Far from Erin's pleasant shores."

Fitzsimmons smiled genially and quoted Dickens: " Lord, keep my memory green.'" Then, a little too hastily for my taste, he made a gesture towards the front of the house. "If you will please follow me, I shall show you the room you have no doubt come to inspect."

Cavendish's study faced east. It lay in a pleasant, mellow light; a great chestnut blocked much of the sunshine, and also ensured that the room could not be observed from the neighbouring house. About a yard from the door, Fitzsimmons pointed to the carpet. On it, there was a stain, roughly a foot in diameter.

We stood surveying the crust of rusty brown, and the butler said: "This is the spot where Mr Cavendish's head came to rest. He was on his back." Then Fitzsimmons gestured towards a cushion that lay some feet away in front of a book case. The cushion showed specks of dried blood, as well as a hole through which some of the stuffing protruded. "The cushion was next to the body."

"Did the shot kill him immediately?" Holmes asked no one in particular.

The butler replied: "Yes, Dr Lanyon said that was certainly the case. It appears the bullet passed through Mr Cavendish's brain and then lodged in his spinal column. Life must have been eclipsed instantaneously."

I could not help but note the calm detachment with which Fitzsimmons reported on his former employer's face. It was on the tip of my tongue to say something to that effect, but Holmes was already nodding in an absent-minded fashion. His eyes sought out the safe, an old-fashioned contraption that stood some fifteen feet away beside a mahogany desk.

My companion looked at the floor, again at the safe, and then crossed the room.

We all followed, and Holmes knelt to inspect the safe's door, which hung slightly ajar.

"It took the fellow a number of attempts to find the right spot. See here," Lestrade pointed to two holes drilled slightly below the centre of the door's right side. "These missed the bolt."

"Evidently," muttered Holmes, then swung open the door with his fingertips. The safe was empty.

"The contents are at the station, I take it?"

"I took only the valuables, that is, the stock certificates," Lestrade replied. "The items of lesser value or of a delicate nature I felt it would be all right to lock away here." He pointed towards the desk.

"May I see them?"

"Certainly." The inspector produced a key from his hip pocket and unlocked one of the desk drawers. Reaching inside, he brought out two stamp albums as well as a stack of sepia-coloured photographs and laid everything on the leather writing surface.

Holmes took up the photographs and began flipping through them. I peered over his shoulder, and I must confess to feeling a twinge of embarrassment. This line of work occasionally affords one glimpses into your fellow men's privacy that suggest a wide margin between their lives as they lead them and as they imagine them. The pictures showed a young lady in various stages of undress and made up to appear as a member of a harem. She was lounging on divans or by Moorish-looking fountains; once or twice, she appeared to be engaged in that strange oriental custom of belly-dancing. Holmes checked the reverse of the photographs for inscriptions, of which there were none, and then laid the stack aside.

Next he began looking through the stamp albums in the same methodical fashion. It appeared the Major General had been a philatelist throughout his long and illustrious career. The little, coloured rectangles came from all parts of the Empire. I saw stamps from East Africa, Gibraltar, and India, and many other places that have come under the crown's protection for their advancement and benefit. The stamps were mounted in neat rows on the cardboard of the album page. Once in a while, I noticed, Holmes would carefully move his fingertips across the gaps between the stamps that signified the as-yet incomplete nature of the collection.

Suddenly, Fitzsimmons spoke up behind us. "Madam, these gentlemen have come to aid Inspector Lestrade in his investigation."

We turned. In the doorway stood a woman in a black silk dress. I recognized Miss Cavendish immediately from the etchings I had seen advertising her public appearances. She was one of those relentless campaigners for the right of women to abandon the safety and tranquillity of the domestic sphere and to venture forth into the tarnished world with which to contend has been the allotment of the male sex. She appeared to be her late brother's junior by a decade, and she had preserved much of what in her youth must have been an astonishing beauty. Her figure still displayed shapely curves, and she stood well over five feet tall. Her features were lean, with high cheek bones and a small pointy nose. Most of her hair glowed a deep auburn, while some strands had paled to the colour of single malt. A bun at the back of her head lent her a regrettably severe appearance. Now she advanced into the room with precise, soldierly steps, and both Holmes and I bowed and expressed our condolences.

"Thank you, gentlemen," she said. "I certainly appreciate your help." Her voice had volume without being loud; I could easily imagine it filling a lecture hall.

"And I am delighted to meet you," she continued. "Occasionally, I do find time to leaf through the *Strand Magazine*, and I have come to admire your acumen, Mr Holmes, and to enjoy your narratives of the investigations, Dr Watson."

Holmes smiled graciously, and I, too—fidgeting somewhat with my hands, I am afraid to say—expressed my appreciation of her complimentary opinion.

"Do you have any idea who is responsible for this dastardly crime?" she now asked in a clipped tone, looking at Holmes.

My companion sidestepped the question by posing one himself: "Tell me, please, Miss Cavendish, why do you believe your brother kept gold bullion in this safe?"

"Well, he told me so himself on a number of occasions, and my brother never made unfounded assertions. You see, Mr Holmes, my family lost quite a substantial amount of money in the panic of 1825, and one of the lessons our father inculcated in us was not to place undue trust in banks or paper money. 'I have yet to see a place where people don't value gold,' he used to say. 'You can't go wrong with gold.'"

"Hard to argue with that," Holmes nodded. "And who, besides yourself, might have been privy to the knowledge that this safe contained a small fortune?"

"I understand why you should ask this question, Mr Holmes, and I've had similar thoughts," replied the lady. "But I cannot see that this line of reasoning will lead us anywhere. My brother certainly did not hold back when it came to expressing his dim view of banks, but the fact that he kept gold bullion in the house he would, if at all, only have mentioned to a few friends. Those would all be elderly gentleman themselves, and besides, the personages with whom my brother was on a more intimate footing are all of sound character and of secure financial standing."

"Sometimes we find ourselves surprised at the company people keep," Lestrade interjected at this point.

Instantly, a deep flush rose up the lady's neck into her cheeks, and she spun around. "Mr Lestrade, there were many issues on which we did not see eye to eye. But this much I will say, my brother was a gentleman in every respect. I have already expressed my resentment at these insinuations that the company he kept was anything less than that befitting a man of sound morals."

The inspector lifted his palms outward in a placating gesture, but Miss Cavendish was not yet finished.

"I believe it most likely that the general air of abandonment made this house appear an easy target, occasioned by the fact that the person responsible for the property left his post." She shot Fitzsimmons a glance that might have chilled a band of drunken mercenaries to the bone. "Unfortunately, my brother returned home while the burglary was underway, and thus fell victim to this hideous crime."

The butler's features tightened in an effort to remain silent, but he could not help himself: "Madam, I have repeatedly expressed my chagrin at the events, and while I admit to a certain amount of responsibility, I would like to emphasize that Mr Cavendish had expressly stated his intention of staying in the countryside till Wednesday. Otherwise, I should never have gone out of town." He turned to my companion, his voice now raspy. "Mr Holmes,

I appeal to your reasonableness. I have been in the employ of the Cavendish family for eleven years, and my loyalty and dedication have always been exemplary."

"That may be so, Mr Fitzsimmons," said Holmes, "but I have a sense you will not be receiving the best of references." He looked out of the window at the houses across the street and continued: "In any case, I am sure we shall get to the bottom of all this. I should now like to have a word with the doctor you called in to help. I believe the gentleman lives close by. Do you think we might find him at home?"

The butler appeared somewhat taken aback at Holmes's brusqueness, but he pulled himself together. "Yes, there is a good chance. Dr Lanyon retired some years ago from general practice. Professionally he is only available to his old friends and patients."

"Splendid," said my companion. "If you would be so good as to lead the way, Mr Fitzsimmons."

We followed the butler out of the house and along the gravel path we had walked up less than an hour before. Dr Lanyon's house stood diagonally across from the Major General's. It was not quite as impressive and lacked a front garden. Nonetheless, the unstained, sand-coloured façade and the wide windows suggested a degree of affluence far beyond that achieved by your humble author in the profession he shared with the owner.

Fitzsimmons reached for the brass knocker and gave two sharp raps. Immediately, a shuffling noise could be heard, and an elderly woman with broad, friendly features and wearing an apron opened the lacquered black door. To the butler's question as to whether the doctor was in she replied in the affirmative. She showed us into a well-appointed parlour that clearly received little usage. The atmosphere had a stale quality to it, and I noticed some dust inside an empty decanter. I had just been inspecting an old microscope standing on a sideboard, when the door swung open and Dr Lanyon stepped into the room with the air of a man in a hurry.

"Good day, ladies and gentleman," he said in a mannered voice, bowed to Miss Cavendish and shook hands with Holmes and myself.

"How can I be of assistance?"

The doctor had a full head of white hair and was wearing spectacles. The blue eyes behind them sparkled with intelligence, and his wrinkled features displayed a scholastic, even monkish appearance. I judged him to be in his seventh decade, but he seemed hale and hearty, and the grip of his hand might have been that of a man half his age.

"Tell me, Doctor," said Holmes after the usual preliminaries had been exchanged. "Do you believe Major General Cavendish was a man content with the circumstance of his life?"

The doctor was, I daresay, a trifle surprised at the question, as was I. While he was tilting his head left and right with the mien of someone weighing a problem, Holmes added:

"You knew each other quite well, I understand."

"Yes," replied Dr Lanyon. "Ever since the Major General retired here five years ago, I have had the honour of being his physician, and I believe I can state that a friendship developed."

"Well," Holmes resumed. "So you should be able to tell whether he was a happy man."

"As I just pointed out, I was Mr Cavendish's physician. I deal with bodies, Mr Holmes. And I can state with confidence that my patient was in reasonably good health for his age, suffering the odd attack of gout, but nothing about which to become unduly concerned." The doctor interrupted himself and seemed to reflect. Then he continued more cautiously: "As regards the state of his mind, I can advance no professional opinion. I will say this much, however: the passing of his wife three years ago was a severe blow. He responded as manfully as you might expect from someone with his career, but you can never tell what lingering effects such a shock might have on the system. Occasionally, he would remark that he missed her dearly, but I'm afraid he never unburdened himself to me."

Holmes eyed the doctor narrowly. "As his physician and friend, shouldn't the whole man have been your concern, not merely his joints?"

At this provocation, Dr Lanyon drew in his breath sharply. "Mr Holmes," he said in a stentorian voice. "As you are surely aware, we all have our areas of expertise. You have yours, I have mine. We do what we can within the confines of our abilities to improve…"

Plainly, he had not yet had his say, but my companion broke in. "I am not persuaded your abilities are entirely sufficient, Dr Lanyon."

I was aghast; Holmes is not the most tactful of men, but rarely in the many years of our acquaintance had I seen him to be positively rude.

"And I am not persuaded your intellect deserves its reputation!" shot back the doctor. "I have seen to tens of thousands of cases in my lifetime."

"Seeing is one thing, Dr Lanyon. Success is another."

"I believe my patients's gratitude testifies to my abilities!"

"Ah yes, gratitude" replied my companion. "Did you receive it in sufficient quantities?"

"What do you mean, Mr Holmes?!"

"We stretch our capacities to the breaking point, don't we, and we have a right to our just desserts. What is that Latin phrase? *Damus petimas…*"

"*Damus petimus!*" shot back the doctor with such vehemence one might have thought Holmes had mispronounced holy writ, "*Damus petimus que vicissim*—we give and expect in return."

There was a long pause in which the two men stared at each other. Something had just occurred, yet no one else in the room seemed to comprehend its full relevance.

Lestrade spoke up to end the awkward silence: "Whatever may have been the Major General's state of mind of late, surely our inquiry is not concerned with this issue. It is the gold and the diamonds that provide the trail we must follow."

"The gold and the diamonds," Holmes said flatly, "might very well be at the bottom of the river. They hold no value to the man who stole them."

Lestrade looked at me confusedly, but all I could do was shrug my shoulders.

And then we all noticed it, perhaps me first, since I was standing next to Lanyon: the colour was draining rapidly from his face. Within seconds it had assumed the chalky whiteness of his hair. To the right of the doctor Miss Cavendish took a step back as if in horror, and the butler gasped. They too were observing the transformation. I looked to Holmes, who stood facing Lanyon. My companion's features were taut, his lips a pale line. Suddenly, he lunged forward. I spun around to see the doctor's hand moving towards his mouth. Between thumb and index finger, he was holding a phial. As if by reflex, I struck out, hitting the side of his hand. Holmes came to an abrupt halt as the phial flew across the room and shattered on the marble fireplace. Instantly, the scent of bitter almonds suffused the room.

The doctor gave a rattling sigh, and his knees buckled, as if a crushing weight had suddenly been deposited on his shoulders. Holmes turned to Lestrade, who had remained motionless. My companion lifted his two wrists in a gesture and nodded towards the doctor. Somewhat hesitantly the inspector stepped behind the shaking figure. He pulled back Lanyon's arms, and after receiving another nod of encouragement from Holmes fastened the handcuffs with an audible click. We all stood in silence as the doctor sank to the floor and curled up into a foetus-like position, while sobbing uncontrollably.

"Perhaps you wouldn't mind explaining what just occurred," the inspector said to my companion.

There was a muffled cry, and we all looked up to see the housekeeper in the doorway. Holmes stepped up to the old woman and laid a conciliatory hand on her forearm; then he led her out of the room. I scanned the faces of the others. Miss Cavendish's beautiful features showed disgust as she studiously avoided looking at the crumpled figure at her feet; both Fitzsimmons and Lestrade appeared almost in shock at the sudden course of events.

After a few minutes, Holmes re-entered the room. "Lestrade, you may want to call in that constable who is standing guard over the Major General's premises. He can keep an eye on the prisoner, while we clear up this mystery."

The inspector did so, and as soon as the constable had arrived, Holmes motioned for the lady, Lestrade, Fitzsimmons, and me to follow him. We walked back into the narrow hallway and then began to ascend a winding staircase.

"Like all servants, Dr Lanyon's housekeeper knows where the master has hidden his treasure," Holmes said as we reached the first landing.

He turned left into the doctor's library. Floor to ceiling, the walls were covered with book shelves, not an inch of open space in them for additional volumes. In the centre of the room stood a comfortable looking, damask covered winged back chair. Beside it, on a small table lay a box of cigars, some matches, and an oddly shaped pair of tweezers.

Holmes stepped behind the chair and scanned the titles. Finally, he began pulling out what I was able to discern were the volumes of Gibbon's *History of the Decline and Fall of the Roman Empire*. He laid the tomes on the chair, then reached into the open space and extracted three large stamp albums. We all clustered around him as he brought them to the table.

The first thing I realized while watching Holmes turn the pages of the top album was that the collection appeared complete. In the Major General's albums there had been the odd white gap between the rows of stamps. In this one the lines of little coloured rectangles proceeded unbroken, line upon line upon line, stamps from every speck of land that was joined to Great Britain by bonds of mutual friendship and common advantage.

In the second album, Holmes found what he was looking for. He picked up the pair of tweezers, and with its flattened tip carefully detached from the album's cardboard a brownish coloured specimen. Save for the fact that it was octagonal in shape, the stamp seemed unremarkable to me. Holmes laid it on the table's polished surface.

"This, ladies and gentlemen," he announced, "is the reason why Neville Cavendish had to die."

Lestrade leaned forward to decipher the inscription on the stamp. "*Damus petimus que vicissim*," he read. "I can't believe it."

"The British Guiana one cent magenta," Holmes declared. "Issued in 1856. You are looking at one of the rarest objects in existence. There can't be more than a handful of them left."

"But how on earth were you able to trace the murder to Lanyon?" I asked.

"Oh, it was really quite elementary, Watson," said Holmes. "You see, I only had to look at the kitchen door to Cavendish's house to understand that we were in pursuit of an amateur. You might recall that there were two marks produced by a crowbar. One at the lock, the other roughly at the height of a man's shoulder. An understanding of basic mechanics will tell you that the most advantageous point at which to situate a crowbar while prizing open a door is the lock. This the intruder understood after his failed first attempt; he had evidently never been engaged in such a task before. My conviction that this crime was not committed by a professional criminal was further borne out when we inspected the safe. There, too, failed attempts preceded success, pointing to an absence of experience. Incidentally, the fact that the kitchen door was broken open also made Mr Fitzsimmons a more unlikely suspect, since he undoubtedly owns a key, though breaking open the door could, of course, have been a ruse. But I had already ruled him out beforehand." At this point, Holmes nodded to the man in question. "I was confident that no person's whereabouts and movements, acquaintances and friends, personal history and character had been more thoroughly investigated by the police in the course of the inquiry than his."

"That is cogently reasoned, Mr Holmes," interrupted Miss Cavendish. "But still, Dr Lanyon would hardly have sprung to my mind."

"A few easy steps will take us to the doctor." Holmes smiled, but without much joy, it seemed to me. "Imagine the scene, the Major General walks into his study, revolver at the ready. The burglar is kneeling in front of the safe, some five yards away. Cavendish was first brought down by a blow to the face. How was that effected? The burglar could have thrown a tool and hit him. That is possible, but is it likely? I should say no. It is not an easy task to throw a tool that distance and hit a man's head. It seemed far more likely that the scene unfolded as follows: Cavendish surprised the burglar, a conversation ensued, in the course of which the burglar crossed the room to be within arm's length of the Major General, and then suddenly, deceptively, struck his blow. But such a course of events presupposes familiarity between the owner of the house and the intruder. Otherwise, it is hardly to be believed that Cavendish, a man who had evaded death many times through circumspection and shrewdness, could have been duped this time. I am sure, Lestrade," Holmes said, turning to the inspector, "that Lanyon will eventually make a confession to that effect."

The inspector nodded quietly, and Holmes continued: "I was pondering this fact of an acquaintance between murderer and victim while I examined what had remained of the contents of the safe. The pictures of the young lady in dishabille appeared to hold no special significance in the matter at hand. We will probably never find out why the Major General kept them. I would guess their age to be upward of twenty years, and they may have had what one might call sentimental value. Things were very different, however, regarding the stamp collection. Perhaps you are familiar with a slight monograph on the subject of stamp forgeries I put forth some years ago. I am therefore very familiar with the value attached to certain of these items, and I could tell immediately that the Major General's collection was a fine one indeed. There were some gaps, to be sure, but here was the result of many years of dedication. At this point my suspicions were beginning to take me in a certain direction. You might recall that I touched the gaps in the album left for the addition of stamps yet missing from the collection. In all cases, the surface of these gaps was entirely smooth; no stamp had ever been mounted there. There was only one exception, where the surface was slightly roughened; at one point a stamp had been mounted there, and had been carefully removed. And this gap was where by the order of the collection the British Guiana one cent magenta, a priceless treasure, would have found its place. At that point the motive of the crime became clear. It was not the gold and the jewels; the murderer only took those as a decoy, to lead the police astray. The true objective of the crime had been the theft of this one stamp, the absence of which might very well have never even been noticed."

"I guess I can tell the chaps they no longer need to keep an eye on ships to Belgium," said Lestrade. "And I better get in touch with the Belgians, so they no longer expect a jewel thief to show up in Antwerp."

"That would be collegial, indeed," remarked Holmes, lighting one of Dr Lanyon's cigars from the box on the table. "After discovering the removal of the stamp, I had no doubt that the case would be solved. That it was solved so fast required a bit of luck. Three things were evident: the murderer was a friend of the victim, he was not a hardened criminal, and he was a stamp collector. Lestrade, you mentioned that Fitzsimmons called in Lanyon after discovering the body because the doctor lived close by and that he was also a good friend of the deceased. I decided to have a look at the man. The doctor had himself under control quite well, at least initially. But after a little prodding, it became obvious that his nerves were frayed. You will recall that I nettled him with that nonsensical insinuation that the Major General might have been suicidal and that he himself had been neglectful of his patient. Perhaps you observed the doctor's reaction. His first impulse was to reject the suggestion. But then, once it dawned on him that there could be hardly any better outcome for himself than if the death should be ruled a suicide, he changed his position and intimated that his friend's grief over his wife's death may have shaken his firm grip on life. At that point, I was sure of my case. I continued the provocation, and deliberately mispronounced that not particularly well-known Latin phrase; it is the colony's motto. You might point out that Lanyon might have simply been objecting to my faulty grammar, yet the force and instantaneous nature of his objection was revealing. He must have reflected on this motto a thousand times, must have imagined gaining possession of that piece of paper which carries the line night after sleepless night. He could not help himself and blurted out the correction, '*Damus petimus que vicissim.*' At that very moment, he also realized that he had walked into my trap and betrayed himself. A fast and easy death seemed the best option."

Holmes fell silent and looked down at the tiny piece of paper lying on the table.

"All because of this," said Lestrade.

We were taking breakfast at our quarters some months later; at the accustomed time Mrs Hudson stepped into the room to hand us each our post. Holmes leafed through his letters without much interest, but stopped when he came to a plain, cheap envelope. He tore it open; it contained a single sheet, which he read out loud:

Mr. Holmes,
    These are the last lines I shall ever write. In twenty minutes, my gaolers will open the door to this cell. They will lead me through a maze of hallways to the scaffold. I will go to my death knowing that I deserve it. I also know that the act I committed was the result of a compulsion alien to my character. This is no apology and no explanation. You are not the person

who deserves my apologies, and an explanation I do not have. Had our lives not intersected, I might very well today be a free man, with years ahead of me. They would not have been happy years, I am certain of that. Perchance they would have been even more miserable than the years I lived knowing that the object of my desire was only a stone's throw away, but yet unreachable. Damned are those who lack good choices.

H. Lanyon

"He believes he had to commit this crime," I said, shaking my head. "Who forced him?! Fate, the three witches, the dark lord himself?"

Holmes folded the letter and reinserted it into its envelope. With a thin smile he handed it to me, the faithful chronicler of his adventures.

When he did not reply to my question, I persisted: "Well, Holmes, what do you think? Why write such nonsense so shortly before your execution?"

My companion set down his cup of tea. "Dr Lanyon was a collector, Watson. Why do you think people collect?"

"It can be a pleasant way to spend your leisure time," I replied with some exasperation, for I did not understand why Holmes was taking our conversation in this direction. "It can also be educational, perhaps even remunerative, if you've got a good eye."

Holmes nodded and seemed to be studying the contents of his cup. Then he raised his eyes.

"You're right, Watson. Collecting can be enjoyable, you may learn many things, and yes, one day your collection might be worth a small, even a big fortune. But those are not the reasons why men like Dr Lanyon collect. For them, the motive force behind collecting is a wish or a need for completion. To own all of something. First editions of all of Daniel Defoe's works, say, or specimens of all the species in a genus of insects, or original Hogarth prints, all of them. Or all the stamps of the British Empire. The objects the individual chooses to collect may in fact be of less importance, but the sense of lack occasioned by a gap in the collection appears to be unbearable. The desire to fill this gap overrides the dictates of a person's conscience, his attachments, his values and beliefs."

"Holmes, are you suggesting that Dr Lanyon is not responsible for his actions, like a madman?! Even he himself states that he deserves his punishment!"

Holmes rose from the table and pushed in his chair. "I do not know. There lies a chasm between guilt and responsibility, which to fill is not my task. I believe that in the future mankind will learn to think with scientific rigour about the human soul. It is a subject worthy of thought. But for now your questions must remain unanswered, old boy."

And with that, the great detective retired to his room, and soon afterwards the sublime melody of Brahms's *Concerto in D* began to waft through our flat.

THE ADVENTURE OF THE LUNATICS'S BALL

by Adam Beau McFarlane

When you stroll through the National Gallery of British Art, you walk through history. Testaments to beauty created over the centuries hang on the walls and stand on pedestals, but there is a darker, more recent history unknown to most visitors. It's the history of the notorious Millbank Penitentiary. Not long ago, it stood on the north bank of the Thames, the same site where the gallery was built and was once the largest prison in London. Holmes sent many prisoners to Millbank, including its very last one. This last prisoner was a woman arrested in a case that tested the powers of modern medicine and almost extracted the ultimate price from Holmes.

Late one afternoon, a knock came upon our door. Our house page, Billy, opened it and introduced our visitor. His footsteps in his canvas boots were light, and his thinning hair and curled mustache were dark yellow. He clutched a strongbox in both hands. "I seek an appointment on a matter that I do not wish to call to the attention of the police," he said.

Holmes ushered him in. "Hello, doctor. This is my good friend and a fellow sawbones, John Watson, in whom I place my strictest confidences. How may I be of service?"

The man stuttered. "H-h-how do you know I'm a doctor?"

Holmes assessed the length of the man then waved a hand at me. "Watson, you're a physician. What are the clues?"

Looking between Holmes and the visitor, I cleared my throat and said, "The top of the stain on his breeches ends in a straight horizontal line, suggesting a coat. Yet, he wears only a topcoat, much longer in length, which should protect him from the stain, meaning he left another coat at work."

The man nodded and said, "A white doctor's coat."

Returning the nod, Holmes added, "I should think so, too, judging by your odour of antiseptic. And a rare antiseptic at that, used mostly at Saint Giles Hospital."

"I am Malcolm Beamish," the doctor said, blinking in astonishment. "And the constabulary does not exaggerate your reputation, Mister Holmes. It is for these powers of observation and reasoning that I beg your attention."

Holmes returned to his chair and lit a pipe. "Tell me what ails you, doctor, and I will make a diagnosis on its criminal merits."

Beamish produced a small strongbox. "I discovered this box in the room of one of my patients, Elizabeth Dayton. Although the box is from an international medical company, I believe its contents were purchased by a Scots physician."

The wooden box was labeled *Materia Medica*. He opened it. Inside was a yellow, chalk-like substance. I reached out to examine the substance.

"Please!" said he, snatching the box away and slamming its lid shut. "Do not dare touch it! Your very life may depend upon it!"

"Very well, then tell us what it is," Holmes said.

"I submit to you, sirs, that it is the substance that destroyed the infamous Doctor Jekyll some three years ago."

Holmes's face tightened, his brow drawing closer over grey eyes.

I laughed. "Don't be ridiculous. That's just a sto—"

"Is it? 'Just a story'?" the doctor snapped. "The patient who gave it to me has disappeared. I can only attribute her symptoms to the germs within that substance."

The strange case of Doctor Jekyll and Mister Hyde was a well-known tale of horror in which a London scientist's experiment transformed him into a murdering, conscienceless troglodyte. Unable to revert back from his "Mister Hyde" persona and unwilling to control his animalistic impulses, Jekyll disappeared.

"Germs, you say?" I asked.

He nodded. "Doctor Jekyll vainly searched for the origin of his transformation, but the science was beyond him. The substance has no miasmatic qualities nor chemical properties that induce the change. It's simply an organic source of food for entities that can be seen under a microscope, entities that were not considered in Doctor Jekyll's orientation toward chemistry."

"Now your patient has undergone such a transformation?" Holmes asked.

Nodding, he said, "She has become something of a witch—violent and full of appetite. She lives with her parents and has no siblings, otherwise I would fear for their safety. Have you studied phrenology, Doctor Watson?"

"Only a very little," I admitted. "My training was as an army surgeon, and now I keep only a modest practice."

"It's remarkable, the re-generation of her skull and facial features. Science could learn so much about the criminal mind by studying this mutation," Beamish said.

"Indeed," Holmes said. "What of her condition before the transformation?"

"Good health, I expect. I recognised what this material was and what its potential could be, but I thought she could be restored to sound body and mind if I could return her to her natural state, just as Mister Hyde returned to status quo when he became Doctor Jekyll again. I thought I could help her. I thought I could control her. Alas, I was wrong."

Holmes said "What crime did she commit to bring you to me rather than the police?"

Shaking his head, he said, "No crimes that I know of, but I fear they exist. As her doctor, my duty obligates me to spare her the risks of the penal system. Further, I cannot allow my profession to become an instrument of the police."

"How can I help you?" he asked.

The doctor said, "She disappeared in Trelawny, and I hope to find her. After two months of trying to diagnose and treat her, only now have I finally perfected an antitoxin. Just as Doctor Jekyll failed to comprehend his condition's origin, he couldn't have understood how to suppress it."

"Are you aware of the asylum escape in Trelawny?" Holmes asked.

"The morning's papers mention it, but how does it bear on my patient?"

"Several residents escaped inexplicably, but a message from Scotland Yard this morning tells me there was assistance from an outsider. Could this be the work of Elizabeth Dayton?"

Our visitor paled. "She lives not too far from the asylum. Could it be possible?"

"To-morrow Watson and I will visit her home. When we find her, we will contact you."

He wiped his forehead in relief. "I pray that you find her before the police catch her in the act of some vile deed."

The remainder of the evening was uneventful, but I woke with a start in the middle of the night. Loud banging and crashes came from Holmes's bedroom. Without thinking, I ran to open his door. His chambers were locked. I bolted to the coat hooks, rummaged in the pockets of his Inverness for the key ring, unlocked the door, and flung it wide open.

Inside, a figure held Holmes down in his bed. She stood on the bed, her boot set against his spine. Raising her arm, she aimed a gun at me. Holmes's eyes were closed, and his body was limp.

"What have you done?" I shouted.

"Calm yourself, doctor. He is sedated by chloroform and no harm has come to him." The voice was feminine, but the figure was dressed in a Norfolk jacket and breeches. From under a top hat, her coal black hair was cut short.

"Who are you?" I yelled.

"Who are you," she repeated, mocking me. Mascara and eye shadow darkened her eyes and an exotic tattoo marked her cheek. "Is this not the residence of Sherlock Holmes?"

I longed to cross Holmes's room and seize the Webley from the top of his bureau.

"Do not step any closer, Doctor Watson. I may only get off one shot, but at this distance, I doubt I shall miss. However, you may cross to light the lamp."

I moved to turn on the gaslight. Full illumination revealed that Holmes's pyjamas were torn open and a syringe lodged into his lean abdomen.

"You injected him," I said, pointing to the needle.

She said, "With the same material given to me by Malcolm Beamish. You might assume that I am his patient, Elizabeth Dayton, but just as Doctor Jekyll had Mister Hyde, Miss Dayton has Sarah Cole."

From beyond the suite's door, I heard the scuffle of lodgers and Mrs Hudson's staff. A fist pounded, demanding to be allowed entrance.

"Not so fast, Doctor Watson!" she said. "Move to unlock the door, and I will shoot to kill. Would you like to go first, or shall I shoot the first person through the threshold?"

"Please, put down your weapon," I said, backing away to the corner, my hands raised. "You have the upper hand, but your illness has turned you into a madwoman. I'm a physician. Tell me about your treatment with Malcolm Beamish, and perhaps I can help you."

She hid the gun in her pocket, her expression now unreadable. "I spied him here earlier today. Malcolm Beamish was Elizabeth's doctor. He turned into her lover, too, after several visits. She was not well, lonely, and she remained in bed for weeks. Exposing her weak heart to him felt natural."

Apparently she read something in my countenance for her next words were, "No, do not entertain those thoughts! The hysterical rants of a nymphomaniac." Her wide pupils burned with an angry fire.

"No, of course not," I assured her, all the while my hands still raised and a commotion growing louder in the hallway.

"Miss Dayton was not improving. In fact, her health grew worse. She could not sleep, she succumbed to bizarre appetites, and her hair grew rapidly. Her blue eyes darkened until they were black as coal. Her strength and agility grew, too."

"Until she became you?" I asked.

"Yes." She wiped her lips. "When he retired to his home at night, I broke into his office and read over his notes. He has other experiments ongoing, other people he has contaminated during his rounds."

"So you injected Holmes to motivate him to find a cure to save his own life?"

She shook her head. "I do not care if Holmes finds a cure or not. I do not want to be cured. Have you ever read Charles Darwin? Are you familiar with his theory of the origin of species?"

Unwilling to digress into imaginative abstractions, I remained silent.

She waved a hand at me dismissively. "I have an inkling that I am the natural progress of mankind. This condition affects my body like yeast turns grape juice into wine. What I represent is a better individual with heightened senses and quicker reflexes, and I am free from the constraints of so-called civility."

"Then why do you torment us with your presence?" My voice was ragged with fatigue and desperation.

She said, "I want Sherlock Holmes to save my life, not by finding a cure, but by bringing Beamish to justice. Otherwise Beamish must kill Sherlock Holmes too, like he will me and the others. Beamish thought he could manage all of his patients, but now we threaten to expose his devilish meddling."

"What do you mean, 'we'?" I asked.

"His other patients that became victims of experimentation. We are united and in hiding."

"How do you think Holmes can help you?"

"Prove Beamish's guilt and send him to jail for the rest of his days."

"And if Holmes refuses?"

"Before Beamish destroys us, we must silence him instead. Doing so would force us into permanent hiding as fugitives, but we intend to survive by any means."

With that promise, she burst out the open window. I gasped. When I ran to the window, I saw that she had slid down a rope to the foot pavement below.

Against the yellow brick of the buildings across the street, her figure was a silhouette, shaded from behind by a streetlamp. As soon as she vanished into the dark, I opened the door then I started to intervene as best I could for my dear friend. My night was spent rousing him to spot signs of illness and urging him to take various cure-alls. When Holmes woke in the morning, I retired to my bed.

After napping most of the morning away, Holmes woke me. We dressed and took a cab to the home of Elizabeth Dayton. Along the ride, Holmes drifted between drowsing and mindless wakefulness. "Tell me again," he said, "what happened?"

I recounted the incident then explained, "I contacted Scotland Yard, but Lestrade wouldn't search the doctor's office. He said the doctor wasn't the one who assaulted you."

He pinched the bridge of his nose and shook his head. "My bedroom looked like a surgical theatre. Did you already say who visited me?"

"The best doctors I could get on a moment's notice, and your brother."

He snorted. "My brother? He must have left before I woke. What did Mycroft say?"

"He wanted the full force of the British Medical Society brought to bear, while I hoped for the best of Harley Street to visit us. Meanwhile Lestrade claims that Doctor Beamish could not be arrested, but would be questioned."

"He may be the key source of information, Watson. It would be best to leave him untouched." With these words, Holmes slumped into the corner and closed his eyes.

Noticing pustules of a rash growing on his cheekbone, I said, "How are you feeling?"

Holmes opened his eyes again, but they were bloodshot. "Strange."

We arrived at Dayton's home, a mews house over empty stables. It was unremarkable from the other buildings that lined the cobblestone street. The air was quiet on a sunny morning. Quercitron drapery fading to blue-green decorated the home s windows. When we knocked, an elderly woman opened the door. "Yes? Can I help you?"

Holmes stared at her with unblinking eyes. Widened pupils caught her reflection.

"We're looking for Elizabeth Dayton," I said.

"I'm sorry, sirs. She disappeared last week—" Cutting off her remark, she stepped back as Holmes walked through the threshold and trespassed into the house.

I said, "Please excuse us, madam. Serious danger is afoot and we must locate her."

Turning around and gazing down at the woman, Holmes's grey eyes fixed on her figure, then her face. He closed his eyes and inhaled deeply, close enough to smell her perspiration and any soaps and perfumes.

"Where does she sleep?" I asked.

She pointed toward a doorway beyond the kitchen. "Through that door, but we have not heard her return for days."

We crossed through the kitchen. A faint haze of smoke still hung in the air from the morning's breakfast. Raw pork offal lay on a cutting board. Holmes grabbed at it with a gloved hand as if to drop a fistful into his mouth.

The woman stepped back toward the door, a hand to her lips.

Holmes stopped himself. "Forgive me. Your stare tells me all I need to know. Watson, the transformation is affecting me."

I nodded to him and said to her, "My friend has the same affliction as your daughter. It is imperative that we find her."

"Who are you?"

Should I reveal our names? Did I want people to question the mind of Sherlock Holmes? What about the reputation of his loyal friend, a medical doctor? I asked, "Do you know Doctor Beamish?"

"You are from the hospital?" she responded.

"No, but we are in Beamish's employ. Please, show us to Elizabeth's room."

The room was little more than a bed-closet beside the kitchen. Although the home had plenty of light, her space was a dark hole. Holmes lit a lamp and stepped inside.

"A hybrid of order and chaos," I said.

Blankets were swaddled into a nest in the corner, and it was filled by a mound of children's dolls. They were decorated in velvet outfits and satin dresses, their hair carefully combed. As I drew nearer, I realised more detail. The dolls were brutally maimed. Torsos were decapitated. Dolls with heads intact were strangled by ribbons, or were blindfolded and bound.

"Heaven help her," I whispered.

Holmes said, "A symptom of the disease, no doubt. The veneer of self-control scrapes away and we see evidence of what lay beneath. It is childhood, and whatever it is a child finds through dolls: love, belonging, companionship."

"Whatever it is, it has been perverted," I said.

"Violence is a symptom," he said and pointed at the door frame. A bloodied handprint stained the wood.

I said, "Dear God, she's already harmed someone."

"On the contrary, Watson. This violence isn't directed outward," he explained as he waved a hand at the dolls. "It's a hatred aimed at her own heart, hating not who or what she loves, but that she loves at all. The disease is fighting for control of her soul, against her civilised humanity. She was probably overwhelmed by the battle within her, so she tried to take her own life."

Breath escaped my lungs. I noted a pooling of dried blood on the floor and said, "Just one palm print, and it's a left one. She tried to cut open a vein, clearly failing, but drawing a significant amount of blood, anyway."

What would happen to Holmes, I wondered, if the condition progressed to this point?

As if in reaction, he said, "I ask myself the self-same question. What happens when you chip away at the patina decorating my mind? What lies beneath?" The pox that speckled his cheekbone now dotted around his eye, poised to cross his face.

Rather than call attention to it, I turned to the mass of blankets. Under the layers stood a doll's house. I asked, "More fixation with childhood, Holmes?"

He extended a hand into the small space under the roof and I thought his hand looked surprisingly matted with hair. Holmes said, "There's something here in the attic."

"What is it?" I asked, watching him pull his hand out.

"Because it's addressed to me, we can deduce that she slipped in and out during the night without anyone's knowledge." He turned an envelope over in his hands, showing his fingernails now were nearly as long as claws. After cutting the wax seal, he slid a folded card from the envelope. He held the card close to his eye, tracing the writing with his gaze, then examining the corners, the edges, and the surfaces as he angled it in the air. "It's an invitation to a lunatics's ball."

A lunatics's ball is a fund-raising party sponsored by an insane asylum. Holmes was not known to be a patron of charitable institutions. I asked, "When is it?"

"Tonight, Watson."

"Which asylum?"

He handed me the invitation. I read it and asked, "Isn't this a public house?"

"Yes, and it's a masquerade ball." When he spoke, Holmes's voice was barely recognizable. Had his gums suddenly receded behind his lips? No, his teeth were growing into long fangs.

"Holmes…" I began.

"I know, Watson. Our only hope is to solve this matter quickly and finally."

After a lengthy discussion with Holmes, I agreed to go the rendezvous myself, alone. Trelawny was as quiet as it was when we visited the Daytons's home. The public house was on a dark street. Inside, the light was dim and conversations murmured in the air. I walked up to the bar and ordered a libation. The bar-tender had bushy eyebrows under a bald head. A Piccadilly weepers mustache swept his cheeks.

"I have good reason to believe you are in grave peril. May I offer you two hundred shillings to close up early?" I withdrew a sheaf of notes from inside my jacket, showed them, then returned them to their inner pocket.

Looking like he'd been slapped, the man said, "I don't know who you are, sir, but you—"

A shot fired from the bar's entrance. Sarah Cole walked in with her gun raised above her head and trailing vapour. "Gentlemen, you may all leave now. Your lives depend upon it."

A mass of people filed in behind her. Everyone at the bar and seated at tables rushed out the door or tumbled out of the windows. Sarah Cole's party all wore masks. Some were mere eye masks, while others concealed their faces or even hid their whole heads.

She walked up to me, her gun pointing at my chest. "Good evening, Doctor Watson. I'm relieved you could attend."

I sipped a rum and said nothing.

Brandishing a violin, one of her revelers began a dance tune. Several walked behind the bar and started helping themselves to liquor. The bar-tender crept away into a broom closet.

"Doctor Watson, where is Sherlock Holmes?" she asked.

My heartbeat fluttered as I lied. "I don't know."

Sarah said, "Then I must await his arrival." One of the partygoers handed her a champagne bottle and she poured herself a glass. By now, the ball was filled with masqueraders dressed as asylum-dwellers. A bald, wrinkled old man wore a grey uniform and carried a rake, even dancing with it and clutching it as he danced with others. Leeches spotted a doctor. A man with manacles loose on his hands gripped the unfastened ends of a woman in a strait-waistcoat.

She wetted her lips with champagne. "So tell me, where is Malcolm Beamish?"

I took another sip. "I do not know his whereabouts either."

"Then tell me where I may find your colleague, Mister Holmes."

"I cannot say, madam."

Anger flared in her eyes and her complexion flushed. "You come to me so foolishly?"

I lifted my own revolver from my pocket and held it at my side. "Sherlock Holmes cannot be responsible for anyone's death. Nor can I."

Suddenly, a small cadre of lunatics surrounded us. They looked prepared to dispatch me. Sarah Cole said, "You will not live long enough to fully regret that you arrived without him."

"I'm sorry to disappoint you, madam, but I'm pleased to return the gift of surprise!" one of the men said in Holmes's voice. Instantly, he clutched her and two others came from behind to manhandle her into submission. Clawing and biting, she thrashed and contorted.

"Holmes! Is that you?" I said.

"It is me, but barely," he said with teeth extended beyond his lips. Long hair grew over his eyes and his face was mottled with scabs. The policemen looked similarly transformed but instead, they had been carefully disguised by Holmes's mastery of makeup and costume.

The public house's doors were unlocked and a mass of constabulary rushed in to subdue the others. I sipped my gun back in my pocket as a struggling Sarah Cole was forced away.

"A word, Mister Holmes! I beg you!" she called out as they pushed her through a back door.

Holmes nodded and motioned to the men restraining her, then he walked up and looked into her dark eyes.

With a surge of strength, she pulled an arm free from a constable. She strained toward Holmes. Her left hand clung onto his forearm, and her head drooped, touching his shoulder.

Holmes gestured to the constable who refrained from reining her back.

She whispered, struggling not to cry. "Why do you condemn my irresistible impulses?"

He pulled her arm against his torso. She leaned against him, resting against his chest. He lifted her chin and kissed her. "There is a wide gulf between justice and freedom, my dear Miss Dayton. Just as Doctor Beamish must learn this, so must you."

He stepped away and let the men grab her tightly again. As they pulled her outside, out of our sight, she howled beastlike in her agony.

Holmes turned to me. "I must be sedated soon, or the illness inside will no longer be contained. If I am not cured, I can only become the most dangerous criminal London will ever meet."

That night, Holmes took a bed at Selfridge Hospital. Mycroft and I stayed through the night at his side. We induced a fever in Holmes by injecting him with a solution from a tropical disease. He lay in bed for days at the threshold of death, sweating and shivering, a thermometer under his arm and his washcloth always moistened by perspiration. When the tropical disease was cured, his fever abated.

"Were you able to discover the antitoxin among Doctor Beamish's things?" Lestrade asked when he came to visit at Holmes's bedside.

I shook my head. "Beamish lied, creating a narrative to justify his pursuit of Elizabeth Dayton."

"Then how did you cure Holmes?"

"The fever in essence boiled his blood, killing the disease, much like pasteurizing milk destroys microscopic creatures."

"I regret that I missed the raid that captured Elizabeth Dayton, but why gamble on such a risky manoeuvre?" he asked.

"She would remain elusive until Doctor Beamish was brought to justice. Holmes, however, could not effectively prosecute Beamish alone, nor would he involve the Metropolitan Police on hearsay of an escaped patient against her doctor. Consequently, our only recourse was to capture Miss Dayton. From her, we could obtain evidence to arrest Doctor Beamish."

He asked, "And what about the others taken in the raid?"

"Lunatics, criminals, and ne'er-do-wells following Elizabeth Dayton's magnetic personality as Sarah Cole. The ones who returned to asylums gave evidence against Sarah Cole as to the charge of aiding their escape. Many of the criminals offered testimony against her regarding crimes conspired to commit together."

"Damned dangerous, Watson," he said.

"Considering our success, I hope you'll overlook the risks," Holmes said, waking in his hospital bed.

Doctor Beamish's remaining patients troubled me. Like Elizabeth Dayton, they did not desire to be cured, yet they were dangerous if left untreated. Their names were taken, and many were found later, law breaking as they were without consciences from the disease rampant in their veins. Some were treated and returned to regular life. Those captured the night of the ball were housed in Millbank, which had already been emptied for its planned destruction. Unable to reconcile the two halves of her psyche, Elizabeth Dayton hung herself in her cell. She was buried as Sarah Cole, a stranger to her own parents, her body unable to heal itself from the dark features, extended teeth, and protruding brow of the mysterious disease.

MUSE WITH SEVEN PERCENT

by Christian Endres

Holmes lay on the sofa all day, shielding his eyes with an arm that still had the belt fastened around it. Suddenly, the detective supinely turned his head in my direction—the first time he ever moved after two hours past—and opened his eyes blinking.

"What is the matter?" my friend asked with enough exhaustion in his voice to last an entire cricket team after a hard-fought league match. The detective reminded me of a tired, once proud lion in the midday heat of the savanna, whose glory days were long past.

I sat on the chair in front of Holmes silently for quite some time, my elbows propped on my knees, face buried in my hands; I saw Holmes through a small gap between my fingers.

I did not wish to see more of him or the world in general.

Frustration had been eating away at me for days and had finally gnawed itself a tunnel to my soul. I had not been able to put a proper line onto the paper for weeks—the inquiries of my agent and my publisher had long since dropped any hint of politeness or concern; they only sounded demanding and threatening now. Even my publisher in the States had insinuated to Mr Murdock and Mr Nelson, my lawyers in New York, that he would not accept any more delay and was ready to take up legal measures, should the new manuscript not find its way onto his desk soon.

But should I have related all that to Holmes? What did he know of the troubles that befell a writer? Had he not often enough smiled at my work as chronicler and considered me with more than only friendly mockery? Moreover, writer's block was no crime, thus it could not really interest the great detective.

Maybe I judged my friend too harshly back then. To be sure, his state—once more owed to his preceding devotion to the hated syringe filled with a seven percent solution of cocaine—was not fit to lighten up my mood. Quite the opposite. To see this brilliant man stretched down on the sofa like this hurt my soul.

"Watson?" Holmes's voice sounded infinitely tired, as if every syllable took more strength than he could muster.

I lowered my hands and looked at the detective with a vacant expression.

"My muse got lost," I answered curtly. "And that even you can hardly retrieve for me, Holmes."

Even if in his state he detected my brusqueness, Holmes took no notice. Phenomenally slowly, he swung his long legs from the sofa and heaved himself into a sitting position. It took him two attempts to finally get up on his feet.

"Lost items are my speciality," he mumbled unconvincingly, before scuffling off to his room on shaky legs.

I followed him with my eyes, grimacing every time he had to support himself on a piece of furniture.

Holmes's befuddled offer of help made my heart grow even heavier and miserable.

There was no improvement when my friend returned to the parlour five minutes later. He still wore his dressing gown and looked like he was the Grim Reaper's brother: his hair unkempt, his cheeks hollow, his pale skin blue-veined and exhibiting a sickly sheen.

"Where have you last seen your Calliope, Watson?" Holmes asked with a quiet voice, but in great earnest. The way he looked, he had at least shaved off his five o' clock shadow. I decided to acknowledge his good intentions and overlook the three patches adorning neck, chin and cheek.

"I don't know," I replied with a heavy sigh. Indeed I could not remember when I last had written something useful, apart from prescriptions for my patients.

"Hm. Well, well. Remarkable." The fever of the hunt usually lighting up Holmes's eyes when turning his attention on a new and intricate case, did not manage to penetrate the fog clouding his gaze. "Then we just start in the cellar and work our way upstairs," he mumbled. When he turned to the door quickly, he started staggering anew like a drunkard and had to support himself on a chest of drawers, nearly knocking down the lamp standing on it.

"Leave it be, Holmes," I begged my friend as gently as I could at this moment. I got up, stepped up to Holmes and placed a hand on his shoulder. "I appreciate it, really. But you are in no shape to seriously…"

"Rubbish, Watson!" Holmes rudely brushed my hand aside; again he swayed slightly. "It would be rather ridiculous, if the two of us could not manage to find such a fickle wench hiding away somewhere in our own house. Come, old chap!"

We must have made a jolly peculiar sight, sneaking through the house like that, with dishevelled hair, in slippers and not exactly wearing our Sunday best.

Mrs Hudson, at any rate, eyed us suspiciously as if we were two gipsies, when she encountered us in the stairwell.

"Out of the way, Mrs Hudson!" Holmes called out in passing and clung to the stair-rails like a drowning man. "Divine beings on the run."

Holmes searched the laundry room and even the coal cellar with the greatest care—without discovering a single footprint of my muse in the coal dust, of course. The only thing he managed to bring to light was a lot of shards, when he knocked a box of Mrs Hudson's Christmas baubles off a discarded wardrobe (which Holmes had to shift, believing a secret door to hide behind it).

"Hmmm." Holmes pressed his pale lips together. The shadows beneath his eyes were as dark as the briquettes he had just examined through his magnifying glass. "The attic?" my friend asked eventually.

I sighed resignedly on seeing Holmes's hopeful expression.

"The attic," I agreed, with little enthusiasm.

But the seldom visited attic above our rooms did not yield up a muse, either, although we were able to secure a few women's clothes—some of Holmes's discarded costumes. In addition, I stumbled into a huge and sticky cobweb, whereas Holmes nearly burned down the house when a match dropped from his shaking fingers. We swiftly trampled out the burning spots.

When to Mrs Hudson's relief—and mine—we returned to our rooms, we tiredly fell down onto sofa and chair.

I recalled the last hour and could only shake my head, smiling. A short glance across the low table between us showed me that Holmes smiled to himself exhaustedly but also with a strange contentedness. The way he sat there—his hands in the pockets of his dressing gown, decorated with coal dust and cobwebs, his pointed chin tilted towards his chest—he looked much more like my keen housemate and astute companion. The haze on his eyes had also lifted considerably.

Suddenly, we both broke out in gales of laughter such as I had seldom encountered with me or Holmes.

"What fools we are, old friend!" Holmes panted between to gasps of breath, while I wiped the tears from my eyes. "Clattering about the house like dervishes, scaring poor Mrs Hudson half to death! We can consider ourselves lucky she did not show us the door."

"It was your idea!" I retorted snorting.

Holmes nodded, all at once solemn again.

"Correct. And I do not regret it," he replied matter-of-factly. "After all, the case is solved."

I looked at him with an uncertain grin.

"It is?"

"Naturally." Holmes tamped his pipe and lit it. The match lay absolutely calm within his hand. All of a sudden I realised that Holmes's voice rang firm and sonorous again.

What was more, my fellow lodger gave me a sincere amicable smile full of warmth.

"Write down this queer episode, Watson," Holmes urged me. "Come! At once! I bet that afterwards the rest of your writing will go much easier. Moreover, your loyal readers would never expect your muse to be that same seven percent solution you usually despise so."

A seven percent solution—or a housemate who was not only the Empire's best detective and actor, but also the best friend a man could wish for.

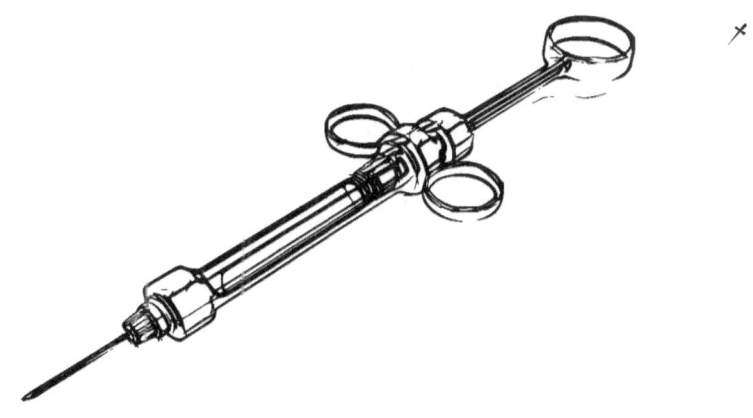

SIMPLICITY ITSELF

by Zack Wentz

Now I mind me own, guv. Ain't the sort to ask favours a no one. Take care a me own business and mind me own. But forty pounds, guv, that's a great lotta lolly to a bloke like you or me, innit. Bloomin' lot, and I says to meself I been bringin' the gentleman 'is needs for so long, what w' 'is reputation and all, I figga askin' ain't so big a thing. Just puttin' a little problem to 'is great mind.

So's I'm makin' 'is special delivery a bit early, few days, all the way from Dover where I'm takin' care a some other business, seein' a elbow relation who makes 'is cake by way a solicitin'. Owes me a favour, 'e does, and won't charge me nothin' for 'is trouble. Any rate, Mrs 'Udson's always a bit surprised to see me, and this time more so, seein' as 'ow Mr 'Olmes din't 'ave time to warn 'er I was comin', but I gots me titfer in me 'and, bowin' low, polite as could be, and she lets me in to see the gent w' just a nod and a shudder.

"Mr 'Olmes?" I says, and give a knock and 'e says enter do please so's I go in and there's the great man 'isself, sittin' in 'is fine chair in 'is dressin' gown, chewin' on 'is unlit briar.

Now what anybody does is 'is own affair, I say. Me, I don't touch the stuff. Bring it to 'im, I will, all 'e likes, but the time I give it a try I thought I was at bloomin' death's gate, 'eart goin' in me ears like it was fit to bust right out me 'ead. I tell you, I can't see the bloomin' point.

Any rate, I says 'ow do you do, sir, still pinchin' me 'at, all 'umble like, and Mr 'Olmes says it's fine to see me, as 'e 'as been in recent need, and 'e's impressed I made it so quick all the way from Dover. Cor blimey, I says. 'Ow's 'e know I come all the ways from Dover? and 'e says, pointin' a long, skinny finga at me gallies, the mud is such that only comes from Dover, particularly since only in Dover 'as it today rained.

Cor, 'e's a remarkable man, and I'm sayin' beg pardon 'bout the mud, leanin' forward to give to 'im 'is special delivery w' out walkin' any more mud 'bout 'is room, right? and 'e looks good and ready to get 'is 'ands on said special delivery, but says we're to wait a moment for a visit from 'is colleague, who will appear presently, and I ain't 'eard nothin' indicatin' anyone's approach, but sure enough there's a 'ard knock at the door downstairs, cheery 'ullo from Mrs 'Udson, more cheery than I got, mind you, and clompin' up and in comes that doctor gent.

Now 'e don't like me one bit. No, sir. Mostly on account a what I bring Mr 'Olmes. Says it's a detreement to 'is consteetooshin, see. Gives me a look down 'is nose, but that don't bother me none. I know 'is type.

"Evenin', guv," says I, but not so much as a sniff from this flash fellah. Like I ain't good enough for 'is eyes.

"Calm yourself, Watson," Mr 'Olmes says, smilin' a bit as 'e says, and the doctor lets out w' a puff.

Now, mind you, I ain't said nothin' 'bout this favour yet. Not a peep, but Mr 'Olmes is still smilin' and says to me I must 'ave a certain thing in mind, comin' days early like I done, and 'e suspects it 'as to do w' some missin' brass that I come into inna 'praps unlawful fashion.

Cor, you coulda knocked me down w' a 'ow do you do. Yes, sir, I says. 'Ow did ya know, sir? And the doctor bloke gives w' another puff, eyes rollin' up like 'e's beseechin' the Good Lord 'elp 'im.

Firstly, 'e says, I'm 'oldin me 'at like I'm chauntin' lay, griddlin' inna street, when usually 'alf the time I don't so much as take it off me 'ead. Second, it's just 'bout time nethers to pay, but I'm usually well off enough to leave 'im at this time alone, spite a that. Third, I ain't yet asked for what I'm owed. Four, I coulda just as well gone to the constable if this money were a thing I came into accordin' to law. All this which leads 'im to believe there's somethin' more, and says 'e could go on, but don't wish to be mutually embarrassin' to us.

Now that doctor chap is 'avin a good chuckle under 'is whiskers, this point, thinkin' I'm quite a mug, but I don't mind it one bit, playin' the fool. Bigger things on me mind, like the missin' lolly, and the lot a bloomin' murderous thugs 'praps out for me 'ead, and Mr 'Olmes says out w' it and let 'im 'ear me tale, so's I starts the tellin'.

So's I'm to earn forty crown, simple thing a takin' a certain parcel point A, point B, right? 'Alf the money up front, 'alf when it arrives. Parcel don't show up by way a me neat delivery, me life ain't worth as much piss you can fit inna thimble (pardon, guv). Now this ain't a problem a'tall. I done such jobs since I was knee 'igh to a cleg, some for Mr 'Olmes even, and I could run that route in me sleep, much as I don't like goin' into that particular B area on account a 'ow nasty it can get, 'specially at night.

First chap who gives it to me I ain't seen in all me life. Coulda been anybody. Plain person you'd see any day. Square rigged. Average cove. Well, I gets me money from 'im and this tiny parcel, little bright box not bigger than an apple plucked down too soon from the tree. Tiny thing, gleamin' yellow and orange, and I'm on the fly next location. Goes off w' out a 'itch. Make the run in record time, right? Few blokes I know try to get me on the way to stop off at the lushin' ken for a quick round, but I wave 'em off on account a bein' busy, them sayin' now they don't think much a me as I go.

So's I get to the place a this second bloke to meet, 'ead a schedule, as is me known specialty, s'posed to be a great gang a 'em w' a big one as don, w' whom I'm s'possed to deal, alley next a shutdown flower shoppe deep in the rookery, and it's good and black, see? London particular. 'Ardly see your arm in front a your bloomin' face. Lookin' down this alley in the dark, sayin' to it 'ullo over me runnin' 'eaves. Cor blimey, if I din't just 'bout jump outta me skin, up pops this grim-lookin' chap, like 'e just come out an ashcan. Dark and gaunt, skinnier than track or rail, and glowin' eyes, whites all ghoulish, and just 'bout can't see another thing for starin' at 'em.

Well, me old 'eart's goin' in me chest like I'd taken a needlefull a Mr 'Olmes stuff, and this dark chap's 'oldin out a 'and like a claw. Oof, those eyes. I coughed up the tiny parcel right quick, spite a me thinkin' it was s'posed to be not one bloke, but one and a 'ole lot, and might well a left w' out the second 'alf a me chink if I 'adn't felt the first 'alf in me pocket jinglin' on account a me shiverin' fright.

"Please, sir," I just managed to mutter, and out comes the other claw, drops the money in me 'ook, then 'e goes, just poof, and me standin' 'lone in the alley there shakin' like a mouse in the coolbox.

So like I said, this is a right nasty neighbourhood, deep in the rookery. Not the sorta spot a decent cove might care to go, day or night, so's thinkin' I might get tapped on the way back to the crib, I decide it's best to stick me brass in the band a me titfer, and then I'm off quick as a wet drink to get meself 'ome and this lolly locked up in me peter 'neath the deb, safe, good and tight.

Blimey, soon as I'm set to turn round and be on me way, up and out the shadows come trompin' a band a thick ones. Nobody I know, and I says g'night, keepin' me 'ead low, but the thickest a 'em, big bloke w' a terrier crop, looks like a right bludger, says that's not so polite for someone new to the area, and 'e'd like w' me to 'ave a word. 'E's talkin' sorta fancy like. As if 'e's 'avin' a bit a fun w' me. 'E asks me what brings me out their way this advanced time a the evenin' and I says I was out to buy a bundle a flowers for the wife. These chaps 'ave quite a laugh at that, and 'e asks did I not know ye olde flower shoppe's been closed up some months now, and wouldn't be open at such a late 'our 'ad this not been the case even. I says to 'im this I did not know, and then the big one says 'e'd be quite delighted to fetch for me a right lovely bundle a flowers 'is own self if I'd kindly provide 'im w' the proper funds, and they're 'avin' quite a time w' me, talkin' down like that, all fancy like, as if I thought I was a real flash toff, blessin' their 'umble neck a the woods by me mere presence. One a the lot chirps up, oy, guv, 'praps this 'ere's the one we're to meet w' Mr M's parcel, and the big bloke 'isses at 'im right quick, shut your bleedin' fool 'ole up.

Now it all comes 'pon me at once I done made a 'orrible mistake. Sick feelin' in me gut, knowin' these is the very fellahs I was to present w' the tiny parcel, but I've gone and sold it to some sneakin', bloomin', scarecrow sod, and if this mean lot discover this to be the case I'm good as brown bread. So's I'm diggin' 'round in me pockets like mad, 'opin' I might 'ave somethin' to give these thugs so's they might leave me alone. A course there's nothin', I shrug, and the big one says 'ow peculiar I brought no money to buy flowers from a shoppe that's now quite gone, you could say 'opin' to buy 'maginary flowers w' 'maginary lolly, and they all 'ave another great laugh.

Well, you can be certain I was shakin' all right then, but I was tryin' me best not to show it, and the big one says to 'is lot, as long as we're waitin' 'ere, might as well 'ave a bit a fun, and then says to me, blimey, that in't a bad a'tall lookin' ring you got there on your 'and, and gives a nod down at me weddin' band on me finga. I sure would fancy a look at that up close, but me eyes ain't so good, and it's so dark. 'Praps you'd be so kind as to take it off.

Seein' as 'ow me gravney ain't worth but a couple pence, as it ain't got no rock on it a any kind, or made a nothin' nice even, I'm tryin' me best to get it off me 'and, but it ain't comin', and as I'm muckin' 'bout w' this ring, the lads ain't laughin' so much now. Gettin' quiet and this 'ere ring is quite stuck. So's the big one, 'e says, looks like you might 'praps be needin' a bit a 'elp w' at ring. But way 'e's sayin' it don't sound much like 'e's talkin' 'bout any kind a 'elp I'd like, mind you, and out 'e comes w' this great, long, shinin' chiv, 'alf as long as me arm, this thing was, and 'e makes like 'e's 'bout to perform 'pon me some a this 'ere 'elp.

Well, me wits, what little a 'em I'm blessed w', 'ave gone and left me on me bloomin' own, this point. I got this soddin' lot a nobblers 'bout to rob me a me finga and all I done is tried to deliver a tiny parcel. Two a 'em grab me arm w' out the ring and finga in question, get it 'eld up 'igh behind me back, right? Other's got me ring arm out and 'eld so's the big one can do 'is bit a operatin' w' 'is 'orrible sticker.

I'm closin' me eyes, grittin' me teeth, gettin' ready for a fair bit a pain. I've 'ad many a good slatin', but never 'ad a piece a mine own 'natmy forc'bly removed. Still, it's a damn sight better than givin' up the ghost on account a me bloomin' delivery mistake, if that were to be revealed, and right then there's a sound, rummy kinda shriekin' cackle, right? Slicin' through the night, and all these bludgers and meself look up and there, as if 'e's on some kinda platform, 'overin' 'bove us all, is the ghoulish cove I'd just got the tiny parcel wrongly delivered to in the black alley, loomin' like a lamppost, and every man jack a us lettin' out such screams you'd think we was a lot a schoolgirls, runnin' 'round like it's every man for 'isself, and I can't say I ever run so 'ard. Nommus! Made it 'alfway cross town full chisel 'fore I stopped for a breather and 'ung there w' me gargler on fire, spittin' thin gobs in the gutter. Never been so bloomin' scared in me 'ole life.

Any rate, I gets back to me crib and I'm 'opin' maybe the wife'll fix me up a bath or 'praps 'elp off w' me trotter cases and give me burnin' feet a bit of a rub 'fore I turn in and catch meself some much needed kip. Right coopered, I trudge up the stairs and calls out for 'er and nothin', sounds like some sort a bustle in the bedroom, so's I knock and says, "Oy, nug, y'decent? Got a good bit a lolly to lock up in me peter." and some more a the bustlin' and I 'ear a bloke's voice in there. Cor blimey, right quick I'm bustin' that door down, jump inna room and there's me wife in but 'alf 'er knickers, cupid's kettle drums 'angin' out for all to see, and the gleamin' left leg and arse a some skinny, soddin', unrigged rat of a man tryin' to squeeze out me window.

She gives w' a yelp and I'm up on this bloody bastard (pardon, guv) and I dunno where to grab on account a it all just bein' naked bloke, so's I back up and give that arse such a kick 'e goes pop right out the window like a cork, lets out a girl-like scream and I 'ear 'im go alla way down and land w' a great, slimy plop. I turns on me wife and she's got 'er 'ooks up inner teeth like she's 'avin' 'em for suppah, then she gives w' another yelp, jumps and runs out the 'ouse, still no dunnage on but 'alf 'er knickers.

Well, I was just 'bout fit to be tied. Mad as a March 'are. To think me out riskin' life and limb for a bit a chink while she's 'ere at 'ome, joinin' giblets, busy makin' a buck's face outta me in me own deb w' some other bloke. Me own lawful blanket. Thought we was 'ammered for life, the dirty puzzle. I 'ad a look out that window and the 'omewreckin' bastard was nowhere to be seen. Look 'round out in the 'all, down out the street, and the bunter wife likewise is off and gone. Neighbours are startin' to poke their 'eads out, murmerin' what's all that racket, so's I decide maybe it's best to go and see if I can't catch up w' me mates at the gatterin' and 'ave a couple drinks to soothe meself down.

I don't 'member much, but me mates all bought me round after round a grog, sayin' she'd be back in the mornin' and if any a 'em ever caught wind a the 'omewreckin' sod I'd be first to know, but mostly just gabbin' on 'bout 'ow some fancy crown rock just been nicked, changin' 'ands somewhere 'bout town as we speak, and 'ow nice it would be to 'ave at such a fine thing and what a great lotta lolly it's worth, on and on, droolin' at the mouth over this coroner diamond, and I says, "Cor, I wouldn't want nothin' to do w' any bleedin' crown jewel named after a bleedin' undertaker." and they all 'ad quite a laugh at me, but bein' so preoccupied w' all

I'd been through that night I din't much mind. "What good's a fine diamond to a man w' out a lakin?" I says, and they got to feelin' sorry for me lot, scraped up a bit a chink for me to go pleasure meself w' a three-penny upright, if I was so inclined, but three sheets to the wind I am, this point, right corned, kanurd, not fit to dab it up w' the finest toffer if she was to appear and carry me off singin' to cock lane.

I'm stumblin' damn near blind back 'ome, up the stairs and blimey, if I din't 'member to lock the bloomin' door, 'angin' open as a fat cove's sleepin' mouth, and I leap in there, shock a loss already soberin' me up as 'alf the things in me 'ouse is gone. Cor, I been burgled. So's I'm rushin' 'bout, and it looks as though it's mostly just the wife's things gone missin', and 'praps 'er and that soddin' bloke she was coppin' off w' came and moved 'er out on the fly. Bloomin' 'ell, the lolly! I lunge under me deb, and me peter's still there, thank Christ, get me little box up out from under, screw in me key, pop it open, and it's gone. Bloody gone! The forty quid! Gone! 'Ow could she 'ave gotten in there? The peter ain't broke, no sign a it bein' bettied, and I the only one w' the key. To the 'aybag I can say good riddance, but now she's gone and left me broke w' that soddin' bastard and I 'aven't the foggiest inklin' as to where they might be found, 'avin' seen nothin' but 'is great white arse.

But 'praps no. 'Praps that mob a lugs came followin', figga'd it was me s'posed to 'ave the tiny parcel, thought 'praps I 'ad gone and made off w' it, watched me trot up to me crib, waited out the row, jemmied their way in after I went off to lush w' me mates, and nicked the lot, makin' it look like trollop and john was to blame. All t'getha got more than a fawny-rig and a bleedin' finga, right? Even if there was no parcel. But who's to know? I wasn't 'bout to go trompin' back into the rookery askin', and if I were to seek out justice by way a the law I'd be nibbed. Any blue bottle'd slap the ruffles on me, 'aul me off to the salt box and toss away the screw.

So right then I thinks I'll make me way to Dover w' the chink me mates give me for a dollymop to get Mr 'Olmes 'is special delivery early, see that certain solicitor relation a mine who knows a bit 'bout divorces and whatnot, then make me way back to town and see what the great man thinks a me case.

'Avin' related all this, Mr 'Olmes is lookin' rummy pleased, smilin', touchin' 'is long fingas t'getha and noddin' 'is thin 'ead. The doctor chap 'as 'is gob 'angin' open w' 'is eyes buggin' out, and only for tellin' the story am I feelin' a'tall much relieved.

"Watson, would you care to reveal the location of the money in question to this gentleman?" Mr 'Olmes says, but the doctor just looks flustered at 'im.

"Well, I suppose this man his wife absconded with was some sort of locksmith. They returned to his flat and robbed the box of its contents. Although by the sparse description of the fellow, I'm afraid it doesn't seem like we've very much to go on. The idea of this gang of thugs following him to burglarize the premises seems a tad far-fetched to me. I imagine they were all still too alarmed by the appearance of the spectral, alleyway character who scattered them to suddenly pursue a questionable opportunity with such deliberate calculation."

Mr 'Olmes lets out w' a jolly laugh and says please for me to 'and 'im me titfer, which I've still got danglin' in me shaky 'ands. I give it to 'im, 'e reaches in there w' 'is long, skinny fingas and pulls out the 'at the forty crown like a magician tugs a rabbit from 'is grand topper.

And I'll never forget what 'e then said, and 'ow 'e said it. It was like bloomin' poetry. Beautiful bloomin' poetry.

"In your advanced state of excitement, as a result of my covert interception of your illicit conveyance, the violent street encounter that followed with the intended recipients, unfortunate domestic discovery upon returning home, and late night bout of imbibing to cap this over-stimulating evening off, it seems you assumed you had performed your habitual sequence of post-caper lolly-hiding with the aforementioned box when in fact you had done nothing of the kind. It is simplicity itself."

And 'e 'ands to me back me titfer and me chink and I coulda dropped down to me knees.

"Bless you, Mr 'Olmes," I says, and the great man says,

"Think nothing of it, think nothing of it, but if you'd please be so good as to excuse us, my colleague and I must be getting on to other important business. A certain exceedingly precious item must be returned to its proper place in the Tower of London. I wish you the best of luck in coming to terms with your errant spouse, and thank you very much for your effective deliveries, of both packages. Inadvertently or not, you've done us all a great service."

And I'm wonderin' what Mr 'Olmes is meanin' at this point, when 'e 'ands to the doctor chap a tiny, bright, yellow orangeish parcel w' 'is long fingas, and flares 'is eyes up at me for just a moment like, and a shiver goes right through me, 'is lamps all wide and white and ghoulish, but this time w' a rum, 'appy kinda grin on the great man's dear old dial.

"I also advise you to consider making use of a portion of your recovered funds by returning to the relative safety of Dover, until the parties that might be interested in avenging themselves upon your person have all been apprehended. I imagine Lestrade is rounding up a number of them in the rookery as we speak, eh Watson?"

And the great man looks over at the doctor cove w' a laugh, and spite a me deep yearnin' to 'ave a peek in that troublesome parcel, I can tell when I been done a good turn, a fine favour, and should mind me own business, so's I mind me own business.

Simplicity itself. Cor, I like the sound a that.

THE BUTLER DID IT

by Herschel Cozine

Much has been written about my good friend and renowned detective Sherlock Holmes. Most of what you have read are my reflections on his remarkable career. For many years I shared his home on Baker Street in London which doubled as his office. It was here that I found him at this moment in his favourite chair, puffing on his pipe, in deep thought, his intelligent eyes focused on a spot on the ceiling.

Loath though I was to interrupt his unquestionably deep thoughts, I nevertheless was curious to learn more about the visitor who had just left. A middle-aged man dressed in a conservatively cut suit and wearing a raincoat, although the weather was fair. He had stayed but briefly, engaging Holmes in a matter that seemed of no consequence to the detective. I had paid scant attention to the conversation. As a rule such visitors are of no interest to me. Still, I was intrigued by the gentleman and wished to know more about him. Holmes had most certainly learned much by observing him, as only he was able to do.

"An interesting man," I said.

Holmes nodded, his eyes remaining riveted to the spot on the ceiling.

"What can you tell me about the gentleman?" I asked.

Holmes leaned forward in his chair and took a deep breath. Taking the pipe from his mouth he tapped it against the ashtray on the stand by his chair.

"He is an accountant. He is a widower with two sons, and his hobby is stamp collecting.

"He lives no more than two miles from here in a modest home. He recently had an unfortunate accident, falling from his horse. Twisted his knee. You noticed his limp, didn't you, Watson?"

I was astounded by Holmes's description. "Yes, I did indeed. But I drew no conclusions from it. You, on the other hand, can tell all that just by observing him," I said. "Fascinating."

"Not at all," Holmes replied. "He happens to be my cousin."

I was about to expostulate when the bell in the foyer tinkled, announcing a caller. Holmes frowned at the interruption, then nodded to me to answer it.

I opened the door to look into the harried face of a uniformed policeman.

"Please, sir," he said. "I must see Mr Holmes at once."

I stepped back to allow him passage. He took the steps up to the den two at a time, reaching the top stair before I had closed the door.

"Mr Holmes, sir," he said with a slight bow.

"Yes, my good man. Chief Inspector Mudd of Scotland Yard has sent for me, I see."

The policeman creased his brow in a puzzled frown. "How did you..."

Holmes waved his hand. "There would be no other reason for you to be here. My carriage is not parked illegally, and if anyone is in need of my services they will come to me directly. Only the Chief Inspector would send a policeman to solicit my help. How may I be of service?"

"Chief Inspector Mudd was most insistent. A murder has been committed at the Barrington mansion. Mr Barrington himself has been brutally murdered. Chief Inspector Mudd requires your help immediately. If you would be so kind as to come with me."

Holmes greeted the news with his characteristic stoicism. He nodded briefly to the constable, who was nervously shifting from one foot to the other, his face flushed with excitement.

"Yes, of course, Constable," Holmes said. "My good friend Mudd must not be kept waiting."

Motioning for me to follow, Holmes took his deerstalker cap from the hat rack and placed it on his head. He threw his cloak around his shoulders, clenched his pipe in his teeth and patted his waistcoat pocket. Satisfied that his tobacco pouch was there, he stepped aside and waved for me to precede him. Together we descended the stairs and out to the sidewalk where a horse and carriage awaited. With assistance from the policeman I managed to climb into the hansom. Holmes hopped in behind me, took his seat by the window and sat back.

The ride to the Barrington mansion was made in silence. Holmes fussed with his pipe, not once looking at the policeman or me. Lost in his thoughts, he seemed in another world. I had learned not to engage him in conversation when he was in such a mood.

Arriving at our destination, we were ushered inside by a stern looking matron who, I later learned, was the deceased's older sister. She led us down the short hallway to the library.

On the floor of the library lay the body of Myron Barrington, a knife protruding from his back. A book was clutched in his hand. His sightless eyes stared at the plush carpet. Although I had seen many bodies in my lifetime, I never became accustomed to them. I stood back while Holmes approached the body, knelt down and removed the book from Barrington's hand.

"A book of poetry by Yeats," he said. "How dastardly clever."

"How do you mean?" I asked.

"It is obvious he is pointing to the killer," Holmes replied.

"Do you mean that Yeats killed him?"

"No, Watson," Holmes said in a voice that hid annoyance at my disingenuous remark.

"But the use of his name is pertinent. Perhaps you are unaware that Yeats's middle name is 'Butler'."

"Ah," I said, catching the significance of his remark. "So the butler did it?"

"That is what we are being asked to believe."

"But you don't agree."

Holmes straightened up, dropped the book to his side and expelled a puff of smoke.

"It isn't possible," he said.

"What isn't possible?"

Holmes pointed to the bookshelf at the far side of the room. A gap appeared in the third shelf, apparently made by the removal of the book.

"Barrington was killed instantly. His body is across the room from the bookshelf. He would not have been able to crawl over to the books, remove this one, and then crawl back. It makes not a particle of sense. This is elementary, my dear Watson. Elementary indeed."

I had to agree. "Then who…"

"Whoever killed Barrington had to have placed the book in his hand. He was certain that we would connect the name to the killer. The butler was being framed."

"Ah, yes," I said. "I see. But a rather poor attempt, I should say."

"Not at all," Holmes replied. "The killer was certain we would see through this and conclude that he was indeed trying to frame the butler."

"But why should he want to do that? And who?"

"The 'why' is simple. He wanted us to believe that the butler is innocent. By convincing us that the book was a rather feeble attempt to frame the butler, we would turn our attention to others. As for 'who', why who better than the butler himself."

"You mean he wanted to…" I said. Confused, I fell silent.

"Yes," Holmes said. "By calling attention to himself, he was removing himself from our list. Ingenious."

"Remarkable," I said. "But he is dealing with Sherlock Holmes. You are much too clever to be taken in by this bit of subterfuge."

Holmes nodded a brief acknowledgement and turned to Mudd. "Arrest the butler."

"Are you quite certain of this, Mr Holmes?" the Chief Inspector asked.

"I will stake my reputation on it, Sir."

Mudd nodded approval. "That is a most compelling guarantee. Now where do you suppose I might find him?"

"He will be in the kitchen explaining to the cook what happened to the knife he borrowed."

Mudd bowed stiffly and departed, leaving Holmes and me alone with the deceased.

"Amazing," I said. "Holmes, you have done it again. You solved the case in less than five minutes."

Holmes shrugged. "Not so, Watson. I knew the butler did it before we arrived here."

"How could you possibly know that?" I asked.

"Elementary. If you were an aficionado of mystery stories, you would realize that in murders such as this the butler is always the guilty one. It is a basic rule that writers follow religiously."

I could only shake my head at my friend's wisdom.

We took our leave. I offered my condolences to Barrington's sister, who sniffed at my remarks and left.

"She had no love for her brother," Holmes said as we stepped outside. "He had disinherited her and was giving his money to charity. He had ordered her to leave as he wanted to remarry and wanted privacy for his new bride."

"How do you know that?" I asked. "Surely it is not possible to deduce this simply by observing the poor woman."

Holmes shrugged. "How, indeed," he replied. "She told me. How else would one know?"

We arrived back at Holmes's residence as night was falling. A light fog had settled over the neighborhood. Holmes paid the hansom driver and we trudged up the short walk to his doorstep.

As Holmes was fumbling with the key, a shadow fell across the shades in the library window. I nudged Holmes. "We have a visitor."

Holmes peeked through a crack at the figure. "A ballerina," he said.

"Ballerina? Holmes, I must ask how you came to that conclusion."

He turned away from the window and put the key in the lock. "The tilt of her chin. The arch of her back. The way she moves when she walks."

I nodded.

"And then," he added, "there's the tutu and the ballet slippers."

As always I was impressed by his deductive powers. But there was another mystery which I was tempted to pose to Holmes. How did the lady get into the house?

I resisted the temptation. I was certain that his explanation would be profound and, quite frankly, a little wearisome. There are times when silence is truly golden. I said nothing.

✗

THE CASE OF THE TARLETON MURDERS

by Jack Grochot

Now living back at Baker Street with my fellow-lodger Sherlock Holmes, I awoke early on this particular morning in 1895 with an ache in my left shoulder, where the Jezail bullet struck and shattered the bone during my service in the Afghanistan campaign. Holmes already had finished breakfast, evidenced by the crumbs scattered on his plate, and had gone off to the hospital chemistry laboratory to achieve a breakthrough in his latest scientific experiment, or so said the note protruding from under the lid of the half-empty coffee pot. Still lingering, the dull pain in my shoulder brought me thoughts of Murray, my brave orderly in the war, who saved me from falling into the hands of the treacherous Ghazis. Where was Murray today, I wondered, as I flipped Holmes's note onto the tabletop and saw, on the reverse side, an invitation to join him to witness his discovery.

Mrs Hudson, our landlady, must have heard me stirring, because she soon appeared with two soft-boiled eggs, bacon, and toast, which I ate with haste so I would not miss out on Holmes's moment of truth. I walked briskly part of the way to the lab, which seemed to ease my suffering. I glimpsed an empty hansom on Great Orme Street near the British Museum, so I flagged down the driver and comfortably rode for the remainder of my journey. I made my way down the labyrinth of freshly white-washed hallways of the great hospital, familiar with each intersection, until I reached the dissecting room. This I entered and cut through, because the rear exit opened into the chemistry section, where I had first met Sherlock Holmes several years earlier.

Presently, on this glorious summer day, I found Holmes hovering over a large glass globe, under which was a Bunsen lamp, a sheet of foolscap, and a vial with red liquid suspended over the flame. "Now, Watson," said he, as if I had been there the whole time with him, "we shall see if my theory proves correct. The iodine solution will produce a gas that should form the effect I am anticipating."

In a matter of a few moments, the paper began to change colour to a pinkish purple. Then, coming into view, as if by magic, was a latent palm print, with the ridges and furrows, loops and whorls distinctly detectable now. "Voila tout!" Holmes exclaimed as he wrung his bony, acid-stained hands. "This surely will inspire the tongues to wag at the nascent fingerprint bureau of Scotland Yard! Imagine what this development could have accomplished in the Yard's failed prosecutions of the scoundrel Jeremy Conway or the international swindler Benito Zito. I should think my finding will receive prominent mention in your chronicles, Watson."

Holmes could hardly contain his excitement, so he persuaded me to help carry the glass globe, the burner, and the vial of iodine solution to Scotland Yard, where, with his flare for the dramatic, he recreated the scene in the hospital laboratory and demonstrated the technique for the incredulous fingerprint bureau personnel and a handful of skeptical inspectors. They were astonished, to say the least, at the result. "I shall hazard a guess that one or two of you might find this somewhat useful in the future," Holmes predicted, an understatement he intended for emphasis.

Little did we know then that Holmes's new method would play a key role in the adventure that awaited us upon our return to the flat at Baker Street, a ghastly case that took us to the sleepy farming village of Tarleton in the marshy Lancashire District, three hundred kilometers to the northwest of London.

When we arrived home, Mrs Hudson greeted us at the door to inform Holmes that a young special constable from the distant country town was in our sitting-room with a problem he chose not to discuss with her. "I can't tell you what it's about because he wouldn't confide in me," she sniffed. "His name is Hubert Roddy."

We went up the stairs and into our apartment, Holmes extending his hand and introducing himself. He told Roddy who I was and said I was helpful in many of the investigations Holmes had undertaken. Roddy, standing erect and alert, told Holmes no introduction was necessary because he had read my accounts of the exploits and admired how Holmes had solved the crimes.

"I hope my visit here will cause the same successful consequences in Tarleton," he began. "I implore you, Mr Holmes, to lend your assistance in an urgent matter." Roddy explained that what appeared to be a routine missing person enquiry had evolved into a grisly murder mystery over the last several weeks.

"Tell me more, Constable Roddy, I am all ears," Holmes commented. "I am unoccupied for the time being and a trip to the hinterlands could be invigorating as well as challenging."

Roddy continued: "This is my first exposure to a killing, Mr Holmes, and I am afraid that I must admit I am at a total loss as to how to proceed. If only the victim, James Harley Carroll, could talk, I wouldn't be here to trouble you. But he can't talk for two reasons, the first being that he is dead, of course, and the second because he has lost his head. Mr Carroll, one of our most prosperous grain farmers, was decapitated when his body washed up on the shore of the River Douglas to the east of the village."

"Without a face to recognise," Holmes interrupted, "how did you come to learn the identity of the remains?"

"As I said, Mr Carroll had been reported missing two weeks prior to the torso washing ashore," Roddy answered, "and our town doctor who examined it noticed a fresh surgical scar on the abdomen. He reported that the incision had been made by him when he operated on Mr Carroll to repair a hernia just two months before. In addition, the clothing on the body was identified as what Mr Carroll was wearing when he was last seen."

"Last seen by whom?" Holmes wanted to know.

"By the stable boy at Mr Carroll's farm, a lad eighteen years of age—the person who filed the missing person information."

"Pray tell," Holmes went on, "what have you learned of Mr Carroll's history?"

"He had led an interesting life, Mr Holmes," said Roddy, "and only a fraction of it in Tarleton. Mr Carroll was raised there as an only child. His parents died of the plague when he was in his early twenties, and they bequeathed to him the expansive farm of nearly five hundred hectares. He left it in the care of a neighbour, who treated it as his own, while Mr Carroll went off to America to seek his fortune. He prospected in the western state of Utah and located a rich silver deposit, becoming the owner of a mine and a man of wealth.

"Mr Carroll bought cattle ranches in the Wyoming territory and eventually retired a millionaire, returning to his estate in Tarleton to spend the last of his years as a country gentleman.

"When Dr Brem performed the autopsy, Mr Carroll's signature leather wallet, made from the hide of one of his steers and engraved with his initials, was not in his pocket, nor was there on his hand a gaudy silver ring with the letter C on the top. I have been working on the theory that the motive for this homicide was robbery, but I have no suspects. In a nutshell, that is where the case stands. Needless to say, I am experiencing severe pressure from community leaders and my superiors in the county police force to make an arrest, which is why I am turning to you, Mr Holmes."

"Your dilemma," Holmes informed the special constable, "arouses considerable curiosity in me. But before I agree to assist you in your probe, please answer some basic questions. One, did Mr Carroll have any enemies or feuds with anyone in the village?"

Roddy paused to think, then: "No enemies, for certain, Mr Holmes, but he was on the outs with Mr McNaughton, the local grain merchant, over the amount Mr McNaughton paid Mr Carroll for ten wagon-loads of oats."

Holmes asked if Mr Carroll had associated with others in the village.

"He was friendly with everyone, but he was particularly close to his neighbour, Sir Ethan Tarleton, a boyhood friend whose ancestors founded the village. Mr Tarleton is in extremely poor health and Mr Carroll would visit with him frequently to cheer him up. It was Mr Tarleton who acted as caretaker of Mr Carroll's farm while he was in the United States. Mr Tarleton has a son who lives with him and cares for his needs, along with a sister who lives in the village. The son, Zachary, is very protective of the family heritage and has held the family farm together ever since Sir Ethan's health failed."

"Did Dr Brem establish the cause of death to be anything prior to the beheading?" Holmes asked.

"There were no other fatal wounds or marks on the torso," Roddy responded, "but without the head the autopsy was rendered incomplete."

Holmes enquired if Mr Carroll left any heirs or a last will and testament.

"He was a man alone in this world, Mr Holmes, with no descendants or kin. I personally searched thoroughly his home and effects, but found nothing to indicate who would inherit Mr Carroll's farm and his money. I suppose it's a matter for the lawyers to haggle over as to who will benefit from Mr Carroll's demise."

Holmes concluded the interrogation with this question: "Was the neck wound jagged, as if the head had been hacked off with an axe, or was it a single, clean cut, such as what might be dealt by a sharp instrument, a knife or a wire perhaps?"

"Mr Holmes, it was as if he had been executed with a guillotine," Roddy revealed.

"This puzzle beckons me to find the missing pieces," Holmes said. "You are welcome to have dinner with Dr Watson and me, rest here tonight, and accompany us on the train tomorrow."

Roddy politely declined the invitation, saying he had been away long enough and that he would board a train leaving Clapham Junction that evening. "I had best be on my way if I am to be on time—and thank you both for your attention to my problem," he said, adding as he departed: "You won't find a hotel in Tarleton, but you may take up lodging in Mr Carroll's empty house, because it is still in my custody. I shall leave the key in the postman's box."

Afterwards, Holmes said little. He was deep in thought. Once, he blurted: "As I have said before, Watson, there is nothing new under the sun. It has all been done before." And later, during supper at Simpson's: "As in the case of the killer Jefferson Hope, what is out of the common is usually a guide rather than a hindrance. In solving a difficulty like Constable Roddy's, the grand thing is to be able to reason backward."

That night we packed our luggage while Holmes studied the train schedule aloud. "The train for Birmingham leaves at ten o'clock in the morning, and if it is not late arriving there, we can make a connection to Stoke-on-Trent, then Manchester, and finally to Southport, near Tarleton, a trip of five hours total duration. We shall likely find it necessary to hire a drag to take us from Southport to Mr Carroll's former home."

It was late afternoon the following day when the horse-drawn cart turned onto the long, winding drive to the low Tudor-style house that had belonged to Mr Carroll. Our route had taken us through the centre of the village, with its two-story brick dwell-ings and shops, a pub, a post office, and grain storage facilities all built close together, as if in a city. Outside the town limits, the countryside exploded into vast crops of wheat, oats, corn, green vegetables, and a variety of flowers growing in black soil rich with peat. We could glimpse only the peaked rooftops of farmhouses scattered among the fields.

Holmes unlocked the door, which opened into a foyer with a slate floor and walls decorated with landscape paintings depict-ing scenes from the American West. Beyond the foyer was a large sitting-room with an immense fireplace, above which hung the ant-lers of an elk, plus the horns of a steer and a mountain goat. Book-shelves lined one side of the room, each packed with volumes on American law, the classics, history, as well as fiction and nonfic-tion that told stories of Western heroes and outlaws. The opposite end of the room was a veritable museum of Western artifacts, with a well-worn, silver-studded riding saddle on a wooden rack, a pair of snakeskin cowboy boots beside it, and a small table holding a bulky chunk of silver. Horse tack, a lasso, and fancy spurs covered the wall.

"I daresay the man was obsessed with his life abroad," I re-marked to Holmes, who was seated at a desk, rummaging through the documents on the top. He found more papers in the drawers and was examining them when there came a knock from the clap-per on the carved oak door. I answered the call, and standing on the stoop was a young, dark-skinned fellow dressed in Western attire, complete with fringed chaps and a wide-brimmed hat, and strands of hay clinging to his sleeves.

"Beggin' your pardon, sir," he said humbly, "but I'm the late Mr Carroll's barn hand, Alexander McRae. You can call me Tex. Mr Carroll always did, ever since he hired me on in Wyomin' when I was just nine years old and runnin' away from the orphanage."

I escorted him inside to meet Sherlock Holmes, and Tex con-tinued in his quiet manner: "Constable Roddy said you'd be ar-rivin' today, and I wanted to offer you any he'p you might need to git familiar with the surroundin's. He told me you'd be solvin' the murder of Mr Carroll, who was like the father I never had. I hope whoever did it gits his neck stretched by a rope on a tall tree branch."

Holmes and I were charmed by Tex's unassuming, blunt way. He replied to Holmes's questions frankly and without hesitation. We learned that Mr Carroll had risen at sunrise daily to assist Tex with the feeding of the livestock, then he would return to the barn in the evening to do the same. He usually cooked breakfast, prepared lunch, and cooked supper for the two of them. In between those times, Mr Carroll would supervise the labourers in the fields, walk the trails between them to visit with Sir Ethan Tarleton, ride to town on his favourite gelding, Bullseye, and at four o'clock sharp stop at the tavern for a mug of beer. "I can't disappoint the barkeep—he expects me there at the same time every day," Mr Carroll would jest. One day about a month ago, Tex recalled, Mr Carroll was nowhere to be seen around the farmhouse at the noon hour and failed to make an appearance at dinnertime. Worried, Tex tried to pinpoint Mr Carroll's whereabouts by tracing his known footsteps, discovering that Mr Carroll hadn't kept his four o'clock appointment at the pub. Tex checked inside the barn and found Bullseye in his stall, with no indication that he had been ridden. When the farmhouse remained empty that night, Tex was certain something dreadful had happened to Mr Carroll, so in the morning Tex fed the horses alone, went to his quarters above the stable to don a clean shirt, and sought out the police to report Mr Carroll as missing.

"What Tex had to tell us disclosed a great deal," Holmes muttered after the youngster had gone off to his chores. "I believe I shall call upon Sir Ethan Tarleton first thing tomorrow. For now, I shall resume my inspection of Mr Carroll's effects."

That evening, after Holmes had finished his research, we were readying for bed when Constable Roddy came with news that would keep us awake half the night.

"Sorry to trouble you gentlemen so late, but I thought you would want to know as soon as possible, Mr Holmes, that another headless body has surfaced," he announced. "This one was found along a seldom-traveled path that leads from the outskirts of town past a shack inhabited by the village drunkard, George Beidler. It appears he is the victim, although we have no one to make a positive identification. Poor old George—he was harmless. Who would want to kill him? He could have been lying there a number of days, and if it were not for one of our residents taking a short-cut home tonight, the discovery could have been delayed even longer."

"Take me to the scene of the crime immediately," commanded Holmes, "because there may be clues that will vanish by morning."

We rode in Roddy's surrey about two kilometers on narrow roads and through a small forest, at the end of which was a cart path. When we were near the scene of the crime, Holmes ordered Roddy to stop so as not to disturb any evidence. "As I have observed to Dr Watson on more than one occasion," Holmes explained, "there is no branch of detective science which is so important and so much neglected as the art of tracing footsteps."

"If you walk up the path about a hundred paces, you will find the torso all in a heap in a dried pool of blood," Roddy advised. Holmes instructed both of us to remain in the surrey while he took a lantern from the side of the vehicle and proceeded up the path in the moonlight. We could see the glow of the lantern when he reached the site. The lantern remained stationary a few moments, then circled to the left and to the right, then back to the left, pausing for a length of time. Then the lantern traveled farther up the path about twenty paces and into the forest, where it disappeared from view for a short time.

When he returned, Holmes asked Roddy if the person who notified him of the crime had been on horseback, and Roddy answered in the affirmative. "That accounts for the hoof prints, then," Holmes said, adding: "There are three distinct sets of footprints. One set led away from the village, the footprints left by the victim. The second set belonged to you, Constable Roddy. And the last belonged to the killer. He is six feet tall and weighs approximately two hundred pounds. I determined this from the length of his stride and the depth of the track in the soft soil. He wears a new square-toed boot, size eleven, with cleats on the heels. He made his escape in a wagon under the cover of the forest. I lost the tracks of the wagon there."

"But what of the motive, Mr Holmes?" Roddy wanted to know. "No one would steal from a drunkard—George had no valuables. He played cards at the pub for money to buy whisky. Could the culprit be a maniac who strikes at random for the thrill of it?"

"The motive is not clear to me yet, but I have a suspicion. However, it is too premature to discuss," Holmes answered as we drove away. "You can arrange to have the torso removed to the doctor's office. I have seen all there is to see here."

After we arrived back at the farmhouse, Roddy excused himself to take care of matters at the scene of the crime, so Holmes and I went inside to change into our bed clothes. I retired for the night, but Holmes climbed into his purple dressing-gown, lapsed into a chair with his elbows on the arms, his fingertips together, and his eyes to the ceiling.

I awoke in the morning to the sound of Holmes talking to Tex in the kitchen. They were preparing breakfast with a half-dozen fresh eggs Tex had gathered from the hen house and sausages they had retrieved from the ice chest. Holmes informed Tex of the horrible finding on the cart path the night before, and Tex reacted with a wide-eyed expression. "The monster just left him there for the buzzards, eh?" Tex said. "Constable Roddy said Mr Carroll was dumped in the river from the bridge for the fish to eat. There was a blood stain on the railin'."

I also learned from their conversation that Tex would take Holmes on a buckboard into the village so Holmes could speak with the blacksmith, then over to the shack of the drunkard George, and then on to the home of Sir Ethan Tarleton.

I volunteered to clean up after them so they would not be delayed. I planned to walk the grounds afterwards to take in the warm sunshine and inspect the lay of the land.

"This is stimulatin'—bein' with you while you solve the murders," Tex said to Holmes as they seated themselves on the wagon. "Do you suppose ole George and Mr Carroll are lookin' down with pride from heaven? That's where they must be. Neither of 'em ever hurt a soul while they was on this earth."

Holmes assured Tex that George and Mr Carroll had gone to their rewards, and the two consulting detectives went off, smiling broadly. I soon finished work in the kitchen, took up my walking stick, and began to stroll through the property. The horses cropping grass in the lush pasture picked up their heads and followed me for some distance along the barbed-wire fence line. They were magnificent, muscled creatures that Mr Carroll had brought with him from the Wyoming territory, which had attained statehood in 1890, the year he left for Europe with Tex. One red roan mustang, when I reached the place where the fence turned at a right angle, snorted and stomped the ground just beyond the corner. Something there had disturbed the animal, and I went over to investigate. To my amazement, there was a patch of sod discoloured with what appeared to be dried blood near the base of a fence post.

Could this be the spot where Mr Carroll lost his life? I wondered. Holmes, I was certain, would be intrigued by what I had found and would want to see it for himself, so I marked the location with my bowler by placing it atop the post. I continued walking until I reached a neighbouring barnyard, then reversed my direction when a tall, sturdy man about the age of thirty emerged from the grey, frame farmhouse to warn me in an unfriendly voice that I was trespassing on his land. I apologized and quickly made my way back onto the property of Mr Carroll. I attributed his demeanor to the fear the residents must have shared because a killer was prowling among them.

I took a different route back to our quarters, and when I entered, the Carroll home was unoccupied. Since Holmes and Tex had not yet returned, I decided to busy myself with some reading from the bookshelves in the sitting-room. I studied the titles in the classics section, and one volume in particular caught my eye, *Shakespeare Analysed*, by the British playwright Sidney Humphries. I took it down from the shelf, and to my surprise, the gap it left revealed the dial to a safe in the wall. How fascinating, I thought. "Holmes will be enthralled with yet this second discovery of mine," I said aloud to myself. My inquisitiveness was heightened further when I learned that a button on the shelf, when depressed, caused the entire bookcase to swing away from the wall to allow access to the small hide-away safe. I returned the bookcase to its normal position.

I tried to concentrate on the book I had selected, but my anticipation of telling Holmes about my detective work prevented me from absorbing the words. So, I put *Shakespeare Analysed* back on the shelf. I began to pace back-and-forth across the room, much like Holmes's habit when lost in thought.

Finally, at about two o'clock, I heard the horses and buckboard arrive at the front gate. Holmes came into the farmhouse alone, while Tex went on toward the barn to unhitch the wagon and cool down the team. "Tex is a talker, to be sure," Holmes started to say, but I interrupted him to tell him my news about the discoloured patch on the trail.

"Excellent, Watson!" he exclaimed. "It fits perfectly into my theory of this case! Now to the bookcase. Tex advised me that Mr Carroll kept important documents and Yankee dollars in a safe hidden behind the shelves."

I was crestfallen, and my disappointment was obvious. "I discovered the safe while you were gone, and I wanted to shock you with it," I informed Holmes when he asked me if he had said something to offend me. I showed Holmes the button and he pressed it. The safe now exposed, Holmes placed his ear tightly against the door and began to turn the dial to the right and to the left. I knew he was proficient in the skills of a burglar, but I had been unaware that safecracking was a part of his repertoire. "I heard the tumblers click," he whispered after a few moments. He turned the handle and the safe opened. "Halloa!" he blurted.

Holmes marveled at the contents. There was fifty thousand dollars in cash, deeds to all of Mr Carroll's properties, a document from an orphanage in Wyoming, a carbonated copy of a forty-year-old agreement between Mr Carroll and Sir Ethan Tarleton, bank deposit slips, plus a will enscrolled with a date after Mr Carroll had relocated to the farmhouse outside the village. "I was convinced a man of his stature would be careful to maintain such records," Holmes stated. "The only question was where." Holmes carried the documents to the desk, organised the papers that were already on it, and sat to examine the new ones, I looking over his shoulder. He fished inside his jacket pocket, withdrew his clay pipe and a pouch of shag tobacco, filled the pipe half way, lit it, and settled against the back of the chair. The smoke curled to the ceiling as Holmes read voraciously. "This means Mr Carroll adopted Tex when he was thirteen years old, just before they sailed for England," Holmes summarised. "And he has bequeathed to Tex all worldly possessions. We must inform Tex promptly."

We went to the barn as Tex was feeding the horses their evening meal. He was startled and befuddled by the information.

"Golllleee," he intoned. "Now I know why he treated me like a son. But why do you suppose Mr Carroll kept it such a secret?"

"I don't know for certain, Tex," Holmes replied, "but perhaps he wanted to avoid you becoming haughty and arrogant, like the disposition we found in the son of Sir Ethan Tarleton. Whatever the answer, your adoptive father took the secret to his grave."

"This changes everythin'," Tex went on. "I have greater responsibilities now. I'm not sure I can handle them."

"You have a few years to prepare," Holmes added. "The will stipulates you inherit Mr Carroll's wealth and properties when you reach the age of twenty-one. For the time being, it is all in the hands of a trustee in America."

We all returned to the farmhouse for supper, and Tex peppered Holmes with questions about the future. "Right now," he said, "there's the matter of payin' the field hands. And to be honest, I'm a little short of money myself."

Holmes told him there was enough in the safe to care for those needs. "With guidance from the trustee, you will have no worries," Holmes said.

After we ate and were refreshed, Holmes asked me to lead him to the patch of sod with the suspected blood stain. "There is ample sunlight left to go there, perform a test, and be back here before dark," he surmised. Although I was tired, I agreed, and we set off on foot toward the post where I hung the derby. Under the evening sun, the spot was less pronounced than in the morning. Holmes produced a leather case from his jacket pocket, and inside were several small vials containing various liquids. He removed one from the case, plucked a few blades of grass from the stained patch, and immersed them into the clear solution in the vial. "If the liquid turns yellow, then it is blood on the grass," he informed me. It did. "Mr Carroll met his end here, then," Holmes conjectured, "before he reached the home of Sir Ethan Tarleton." Holmes pointed over the rise ahead and said the Tarleton farm laid just beyond it.

"Then it was someone from the Tarleton homestead who shooed me away today," I mentioned to him, and I told him of my encounter with the tall, sturdy fellow.

"More than likely that was Sir Ethan's son, Zachary," Holmes guessed. "I, too, found him unfriendly. He erroneously advised me that by living in the Carroll farmhouse I was trespassing on land that rightfully belonged to his father now. He contended the written agreement between his father and Mr Carroll spelled out the ownership in no uncertain terms." Holmes said Sir Ethan Tarleton was of little help in the investigation because he suffered from dementia and had a weak heart that kept him bedfast most of the time. "His memory is dysfunctional," Holmes revealed during our walk back to Mr Carroll's farmhouse.

At mid-morning the next day, Holmes and Tex took the buckboard to the office of the magistrate, the keeper of records for the county. On the way, they were to pick up Constable Roddy, who would obtain a writ to gain possession of the original of the old agreement between Mr Carroll and Sir Ethan Tarleton. Holmes suspected the agreement on file with the magistrate might have been altered recently. "I shall explain when I return with the document," Holmes said when I went to the front gate to see them off.

To pass the time while they were gone, I opened the volume entitled *Shakespeare Analysed* and was soon mesmerised, acquiring the knowledge for the first time that there existed a hypothesis that The Bard was not a single person but actually a collection of playwrights using the pseudonym William Shakespeare. I thought it preposterous, recounting in my head many of the quotations from the dramas and trying to imagine that they were the handiwork of more than one genius. Time passed quickly, for I was still absorbed in the author's analysis when Holmes, Roddy, and Tex walked through the door in the middle of the afternoon.

"It is as I suspected, Watson," Holmes announced. "Take the carbonated copy of the agreement from the desk and compare it to the original. A page has been substituted which contradicts what is in the copy. Notice the watermark—the depiction of the fool in the floppy cock's comb cap and the collar with five peaks, each bearing a jingle bell. He is in a different position on the bogus page of the original. The fool is at the centre right on the other three genuine pages, and at the bottom left on the substituted page.

"I refer you to my monograph on the subject of dating documents. The McKean Paper Mill moved the location of the watermark to the bottom left just two years ago, meaning the forged page was inserted recently."

What Holmes alleged was correct when I compared the two documents. The bogus page specified that Mr Carroll's five hundred hectares would revert to the ownership of Sir Ethan Tarleton and his heirs if Mr Carroll preceded him in death, whereas the copy made no mention of such a succession.

"Now to prove the identity of the counterfeiter," Holmes declared. "I borrowed from the village doctor a Bunsen burner and gas canister on our way back here, Watson. And that glass globe covering the clock on the mantle should do the trick, if you wouldn't mind fetching it down." Holmes then took a vial with his furtive iodine solution from the leather case in his jacket pocket, set up his laboratory on the kitchen table, and placed the questioned page under the glass after igniting the burner and adjusting the vial on the little stand he also brought with him. "You will soon see the latent fingerprints and hand print of the wrongdoer," Holmes advised Roddy as the forged page began to change colour. Roddy watched in awe as the heel print of a right hand appeared on the margin, along with three fingerprints at the top left corner. Said Holmes: "All that is left to do is contrast these with the prints of young Zachary Tarleton, which we can do with a writ and some printer's ink we acquire from the village weekly newspaper."

Tex, who was equally astounded by the development, drove Roddy to the village to do his part. Meanwhile, Holmes and I discussed the implications of the findings over a bottle of port wine we took from Mr Carroll's rack in the dining room.

It was drawing toward evening when Roddy returned in his surrey. Tex had already arrived in the otherwise empty buckboard and was putting up the team. Holmes and I climbed onto the surrey behind Roddy, who drove toward the Tarletons's home.

Zachary Tarleton was obstinate, but he reluctantly allowed Holmes to smear the ink on his hands and make an impression of them on a sheet of foolscap—after Roddy served young Tarleton with the writ. "What are you trying to prove with this?" he demanded.

"We shall let you know in the morning after we compare your prints to those we recovered from the agreement between your father and Mr Carroll," Holmes answered.

"How can you recover my prints from an old document that was signed before I was born?" Tarleton wanted to know.

"I employ a foolproof method," Holmes informed him.

"Your method is pure madness," he retorted, and strode off to the kitchen to wash away the ink, his robust arms outstretched.

After we arrived back at Mr Carroll's home, we ate a plate of beef stew that Tex had prepared in our absence, left over from the pot roast dinner we had the night before.

"Mr Carroll, er, my father, taught me to cook," Tex said, "but I don't do as well with the stove as him. My stew will go down easy, though, especially when you're as hungry as we all are."

Holmes was in no rush to make the comparisons, convinced that the two sets of prints would match. So confident was he that he relinquished the honour to Roddy, handing him a magnifying glass and seating him at the desk in the sitting-room. Roddy studied the prints thoroughly and eventually disclosed his conclusion: "They are a perfect layover, Mr Holmes. Where do we go from here?"

Holmes said he would confront young Tarleton in the morning but wanted to do it alone. "He might say some things to me that he would not in your presence, Constable Roddy."

"Well, if you say so," Roddy said in reaction, "but I insist on going along and waiting in the surrey outside the house in the event he decides to fight."

"I should like to be there as well," I chimed in.

Holmes agreed, and the next day we set out together for the Tarleton homestead. Roddy stopped the surrey out of view of the front door, and Holmes approached it on foot from about two hundred paces away. Once we were certain he was safely inside, Roddy drew the surrey closer to the house.

Holmes had disappeared for nearly an hour. When he came out, he was escorting Zachary Tarleton to the surrey. Young Tarleton looked disheveled and was bleeding from a gash on his cheek. "Standing before you," Holmes said matter-of-factly, "is the forger who murdered the respected James Harley Carroll as well as the drunkard George Beidler in cold blood. Young Mr Tarleton here has admitted to it." Roddy was flabbergasted. I, on the contrary, had come to expect such pronouncements. Roddy clasped irons on the reprobate and seated him in the back of the surrey between myself and Holmes, then we headed in the direction of the village.

Later, after the prisoner had been secured in the tiny gaol, Roddy drove us to the Carroll home, where Tex greeted the news with a whoop. "Do you suppose they'll string him up before long?" he asked Holmes and Roddy.

"First there is the matter of a fair trial," Roddy cautioned.

"Right after that, then?" Tex pleaded.

"Perhaps then," Holmes responded.

"How did you catch him, Mr Holmes?" Tex continued.

Holmes explained to all of us then the phases of his investigation. First, there was the killer's boot prints near the body of Beidler. "Young Tarleton wears a pair exactly as I described," Holmes told us. Second, when Holmes examined the crime scene, he found in the woods the iron rim from a wagon wheel. "The village blacksmith informed me that he had repaired a wagon wheel with a missing rim for young Tarleton that very morning, after the discovery of Beidler's torso," Holmes went on. Additionally, Holmes said, he learned in the village that the muscular Mr Tarleton was an expert with a sabre, having been taught by his grandfather, the son of Sir Banastre Tarleton, nicknamed The Butcher. Sir Banastre cut off the heads of his enemies with one swipe of a sabre in the American War of Independence.

"When I confronted Tarleton with this information, and the fact that we had proof he had forged the agreement," Holmes said, "Tarleton became enraged and lunged for one of the crossed sabres above the fireplace. 'You know too much, Holmes, so it's off with your head also,' he sputtered. I dodged his advance and took down the other broadsword. He attacked, and I parried. We were engaged in this combat for only a minute when I intercepted a thrust and disarmed him, placing the tip of my blade against his chest. I asked him then what he had done with the heads of Mr Carroll and George Beidler, and he confessed that he had buried them in the family cemetery behind his home. He also acknowledged that he had taken Beidler's life merely as a diversion to throw off suspicions in the death of Mr Carroll, as was my belief from the start."

"That means he killed ole George for nothin' and he killed Mr Carroll to inherit this farm," Tex added. "Hangin' ain't good enough for him."

THE FIELD BAZAAR

by Sir Arthur Conan Doyle

"I should certainly do it," said Sherlock Holmes.

I started at the interruption, for my companion had been eating his breakfast with his attention entirely centred upon the paper which was propped up by the coffee pot. Now I looked across at him to find his eyes fastened upon me with the half-amused, half-questioning expression which he usually assumed when he felt that he had made an intellectual point.

"Do what?" I asked.

He smiled as he took his slipper from the mantelpiece and drew from it enough shag tobacco to fill the old clay pipe with which he invariably rounded off his breakfast.

"A most characteristic question of yours, Watson," said he. "You will not, I am sure, be offended if I say that any reputation for sharpness which I may possess has been entirely gained by the admirable foil which you have made for me. Have I not heard of débutantes who have insisted upon plainness in their chaperones? There is a certain analogy."

Our long companionship in the Baker Street rooms had left us on those easy terms of intimacy when much may be said without offence. And yet I acknowledge that I was nettled at his remark.

"I may be very obtuse," said I, "but I confess that I am unable to see how you have managed to know that I was... I was..."

"Asked to help in the Edinburgh University Bazaar."

"Precisely. The letter has only just come to hand, and I have not spoken to you since."

"In spite of that," said Holmes, leaning back in his chair and putting his finger tips together, "I would even venture to suggest that the object of the bazaar is to enlarge the University cricket field."

I looked at him in such bewilderment that he vibrated with silent laughter.

"The fact is, my dear Watson, that you are an excellent subject," said he. "You are never blasé. You respond instantly to any external stimulus. Your mental processes may be slow but they are never obscure, and I found during breakfast that you were easier reading than the leader in *The Times* in front of me."

"I should be glad to know how you arrived at your conclusions," said I.

"I fear that my good nature in giving explanations has seriously compromised my reputation," said Holmes. "But in this case the train of reasoning is based upon such obvious facts that no credit can be claimed for it. You entered the room with a thoughtful expression, the expression of a man who, is debating some point in his mind. In your hand you held a solitary letter. Now last night you retired in the best of spirits, so it was clear that it was this letter in your hand which had caused the change in you."

"This is obvious."

"It is all obvious when it is explained to you. I naturally asked myself what the letter could contain which might have this effect upon you. As you walked you held the flap side of the envelope towards me, and I saw upon it the same shield-shaped device which I have observed upon your old college cricket cap. It was clear, then, that the request came from Edinburgh University—or from some club connected with the University. When you reached the table you laid down the letter beside your plate with the address upper-most, and you walked over to look at the framed photograph upon the left of the mantelpiece."

It amazed me to see the accuracy with which he had observed my movements. "What next?" I asked.

"I began by glancing at the address, and I could tell, even at the distance of six feet, that it was an unofficial communication. This I gathered from the use of the word 'Doctor' upon the address, to which, as a Bachelor of Medicine, you have no legal claim. I knew that University officials are pedantic in their correct use of titles, and I was thus enabled to say with certainty that your letter was unofficial. When on your return to the table you turned over your letter and allowed me to perceive that the enclosure was a printed one, the idea of a bazaar first occurred to me. I had already weighed the possibility of its being a political communication, but this seemed improbable in the present stagnant condition of politics.

"When you returned to the table your face still retained its expression, and it was evident that your examination of the photograph had not changed the current of your thoughts. In that case it must itself bear upon the subject in question. I turned my attention to the photograph therefore, and saw at once that it consisted of yourself as a member of the Edinburgh University Eleven, with the pavilion and cricket-field in the background. My small experience of cricket clubs has taught me that next to churches and cavalry ensigns they are the most debt-laden things upon earth. When upon your return to the table I saw you take out your pencil and draw lines upon the envelope, I was convinced that you were endeavouring to realize some projected improvement which was to be brought about by a bazaar. Your face still showed some indecision, so that I was able to break in upon you with my advice that you should assist in so good an object."

I could not help smiling at the extreme simplicity of his explanation.

"Of course, it was as easy as possible," said I.

My remark appeared to nettle him.

"I may add," said he, "that the particular help which you have been asked to give was that you should write in their album, and that you have already made up your mind that the present incident will be the subject of your article."

"But how—!" I cried.

"It is as easy as possible," said he, "and I leave its solution to your own ingenuity. In the meantime," he added, raising his paper, "you will excuse me if I return to this very interesting article upon the trees of Cremona, and the exact reasons for their pre-eminence in the manufacture of violins. It is one of those small outlying problems to which I am sometimes tempted to direct my attention."

✗